I WHO HAVE NEVER
KNOWN MEN

I WHO HAVE NEVER KNOWN MEN

Jacqueline Harpman

Translated from the French by
Ros Schwartz

With an afterword by
Sophie Mackintosh

**TRANSIT
BOOKS**

Published by Transit Books
2301 Telegraph Avenue, Oakland, California 94612
www.transitbooks.org

First published in France with the title *Moi qui n'ai pas connu les hommes* by
Stock, Paris in 1995
First Transit Books edition, 2022

ISBN: 978-1-945492-60-0 (PAPERBACK) | 978-1-945492-62-4 (EBOOK)
LIBRARY OF CONGRESS CONTROL NUMBER AVAILABLE

DESIGN & TYPESETTING
Justin Carder

DISTRIBUTED BY
Consortium Book Sales & Distribution
(800) 283-3572 | cbsd.com

Printed in the United States of America

15 14 13 12 11 10

CONTENTS

To Denise Geilfus
In friendship

Since I barely venture outside these days, I spend a lot of time in one of the armchairs, rereading the books. I only recently started taking an interest in the prefaces. The authors talk readily about themselves, explaining their reasons for writing the book. This surprises me: surely it was more usual in that world than in the one in which I have lived for people to pass on the knowledge they had acquired? They often seem to feel the need to emphasise that they wrote the book not out of vanity, but because someone asked them to, and that they had thought about it long and hard before accepting. How strange! It suggests that people were not avid to learn, and that you had to apologise for wanting to convey your knowledge. Or, they explain why they felt it was appropriate to publish a new translation of Proust, because previous efforts, laudable though they may be, lacked something or other. But why translate when it must have been so easy to learn different languages and read anything you wanted directly? These things leave me utterly baffled. True, I am extremely ignorant: apparently, I know even less of these matters than I thought I did. The authors express their gratitude to those who taught them, who opened the door to this or that avenue of knowledge, and, because I have absolutely no idea what they're talking about, I usually read these words with a degree of indifference. But suddenly, yesterday, my eyes filled with tears; I thought of Anthea, and was overcome by a tremendous wave of grief. I could picture her, sitting on the edge of a mattress, her knees to one side, sewing patiently with her makeshift thread of plaited hairs which kept snapping, stopping to look at me, astonished, quick to recognise my ignorance and teach me what she knew, apologising that it was so little, and I felt a huge wrench, and began to sob. I had never cried before. There was a pain in my heart as powerful as the pain of the cancer in my belly, and I who no longer speak because there is no one to hear me, began to call her. Anthea! Anthea! I shouted. I couldn't forgive her for not being there, for having allowed death to snatch her, to tear her from my clumsy arms. I chastised myself for not having held on to her, for not having understood that she couldn't go on any more. I told myself that I'd abandoned her because I was frigid, as I had been all my life, as I shall be when I die, and so I was unable to hug her warmly, and that my heart was frozen, unfeeling, and that I hadn't realised that I was desperate.

Never before had I been so devastated. I would have sworn it couldn't happen to me; I'd seen women trembling, crying and screaming, but I'd remained unaffected by their tragedy, a witness to impulses I found unintelligible, remaining silent even when I did what they asked of me to assist them. Admittedly, we were all caught up in the same drama that was so powerful, so all-embracing that I was unaware of anything that wasn't related to it, but I had come to think that I was different. And now, racked with sobs, I was forced to acknowledge too late, much too late, that I too had loved, that I was capable of suffering and that I was human after all.

I felt as if this pain would never be appeased, that it had me in its grip for ever, that it would prevent me from devoting myself to anything else, and that I was allowing it to do so. I think that that is what they call being consumed with remorse. I would no longer be able to get up, think, or even cook my food, and I would let myself slowly waste away. I was deriving a sort of morbid pleasure from imagining myself giving in to despair, when the physical pain returned. It was so sudden and so acute that it distracted me from the mental pain. I found this abrupt swing from one to the other funny, and there I was, I who not surprisingly never laugh, doubled up in agony, and laughing.

When the pain abated, I wondered whether I had ever laughed before. The women often used to laugh, and I believe I had sometimes joined in, but I was unsure. I realised then that I never thought about the past. I lived in a perpetual present and I was gradually forgetting my story. At first, I shrugged, telling myself that it would be no great loss, since nothing had happened to me, but soon I was shocked by that thought. After all, if I was a human being, my story was as important as that of King Lear or of Prince Hamlet that William Shakespeare had taken the trouble to relate in detail. I made the decision almost without realising it: I would do likewise. Over the years, I'd learned to read fluently; writing is much harder, but I've never been daunted by obstacles. I do have paper and pencils, although I may not have much time. Now that I no longer go off on expeditions, no occupation calls me, so I decided to start at once. I went into the cold store, took out the meat that I would eat later and left it to defrost, so that when hunger struck, my food would soon be ready. Then I sat down at the big table and began to write.

As I write these words, my tale is over. Everything around me is in order and I have fulfilled the final task I set myself. It only took me a month, which has perhaps been the happiest month of my life. I do not understand that: after all, what I was describing was only my strange existence which hasn't brought me much joy. Is there a satisfaction in the effort of remembering that provides its own nourishment, and is what one recollects less important than the act of remembering? That is another question that will remain unanswered: I feel as though I am made of nothing else.

As far back as I can recall, I have been in the bunker. Is that what they mean by memories? On the few occasions when the women were willing to tell me about their past, their stories were full of events, comings and goings, men… but I am reduced to calling a memory the sense of existing in the same place, with the same people and doing the same things—in other words, eating, excreting and sleeping. For a very long time, the days went by, each one just like the day before, then I began to think, and everything changed. Before, nothing happened other than this repetition of identical gestures, and time seemed to stand still, even if I was vaguely aware that I was growing and that time was passing. My memory begins with my anger.

Obviously, I have no way of knowing how old I was. The others had been adult for a long time whereas I appeared to be prepubescent. But my development stopped there: I started to get hair under my arms and on my pubes, my breasts grew a little, and then everything came to a halt. I never had a period. The women told me I was lucky, that I wouldn't have the bother of bleeding and the precautions to be taken so as not to stain the mattresses. I'd be spared the tedious monthly task of washing out the rags they had to jam between their legs as best they could, by squeezing together their thigh muscles, since they had nothing to hold them in place, and I wouldn't have to suffer stomach cramps like so many adolescent girls. But I didn't believe them: they nearly all menstruated, and how can you feel privileged not to have something that everyone else has? I felt they were deceiving me.

Back then, I wasn't curious about things, and it didn't occur to me to ask what the point of periods was. Perhaps I was naturally quiet, in any case, the response my rare questions did receive wasn't exactly encouraging. More often than not, the women would sigh and look away, saying 'What use would it be for you to know if we told you?', which made me feel I was disturbing or upsetting them. I had no idea, and I didn't press the matter. It wasn't until much later that Anthea explained to me about periods. She told me that none of the women had much education; they were factory workers, typists or shop assistants—words that had never meant very much to me, and that they weren't much better informed than I was. All the same, when I did find out, I felt they hadn't really made an effort to teach me. I was furious. Anthea said that I wasn't entirely wrong and tried to explain their reasons. I may come back to this later, if I remember, but at the time I want to write about, I was livid. I felt I was being scorned, as if I was incapable of understanding the answers to the few questions I asked, and I resolved not to take any further interest in the women.

I was surly all the time, but I was unaware of it, because I didn't know the words for describing moods. The women bustled about, busying themselves with the few day-to-day activities but never inviting me to join them. I would crouch down and watch whatever there was to see. On reflection, that was almost nothing. They'd be sitting chatting, or, twice a day, they'd prepare the meal. Gradually, I turned my attention to the guards who paced up and down continually outside our cage. They were always in threes, a few paces apart, observing us, and we generally pretended to ignore their presence, but I grew inquisitive. I noticed that one of them was different: taller, slimmer and, as I realised after a while, younger. That fascinated me. In their more cheerful moments, the women would talk of men and love. They'd giggle and tease me when I asked what was so funny. I went over everything I knew: kisses, which were given on the mouth, embraces, making eyes at someone, playing footsie, which I didn't understand at all, and then came seventh heaven—my goodness! Given that I'd never seen any sky at all and had no idea what the first heaven or any of the others in between were, I didn't dwell on it. They would also complain about the brutality. It hurt, men didn't care about women, they got them pregnant and then walked out, saying, 'How do I know it's mine?' Sometimes the women would declare that it was no great loss, and at others they would start to cry. But I was destined to remain a virgin. One day, I screwed up the courage to put aside my anger and question Dorothy, the least intimidating of the two elderly women.

'You poor thing!'

And, after a few sighs, she came out with the usual reply:

'What point is there in your knowing, since it can't happen to you?'

'Because I want to know!' I raged, suddenly grasping why it was so important to me.

She couldn't understand why someone would want knowledge that would be of no use to them, and I couldn't get anything out of her. It was certain that I would die untouched, and I wanted to satisfy my curiosity at least. Why were they all so determined to keep silent? I tried to console myself with the thought that it was no secret anyway, because they all shared it. Was it to give it an additional sparkle that they refused to tell me, to give it the lustre of a rare gem? By remaining silent, they were creating a girl who didn't know and who would regard them as the custodians of a treasure. Did they only keep me in ignorance so they could pretend they weren't entirely powerless? They sometimes claimed it was out of modesty, but I could see perfectly well that, among themselves, they had no modesty. They whispered and tittered and were lewd. I would never make love, they would never make love again: perhaps that made us equal and they were trying to console themselves by depriving me of the only thing they could.

Often, in the evening, before falling asleep, I would think about the young guard. I drew on the little I'd been able to guess: in another life, he'd have come and sat beside me, he'd have asked me to dance and told me his name. I'd have had a name which I'd have told him, and we'd have talked. Then, if we were attracted to each other, we'd have walked hand in hand. Maybe I wouldn't have found him interesting: he was the only one of our six jailers who wasn't old and decrepit, and I was probably indulgent because I'd never met any other young men. I tried to imagine our conversation, in a past that I hadn't known: Will it be fine again tomorrow? Have you seen next door's kittens? I hear your aunt's going on holiday ... but I'd never seen kittens and I had absolutely no idea what fine weather might be, which put an end to my reverie. Then I'd think about kissing, imagining the guard's mouth as precisely as I could. It was quite wide, with well-defined, thinnish lips—I didn't like the full lips that some of the women had. I pictured my lips drawing close to his: there was probably something else I needed to know, because I felt nothing in particular.

But then, one evening, instead of falling asleep from the boredom of trying to imagine a kiss that would never happen, I suddenly remembered that the women had spoken of interrogations, saying they were surprised that there'd never been any. I embellished the little they'd said: I imagined the guards coming to fetch one of the women, taking her away screaming and terrified. Sometimes, the woman was never seen again, sometimes she'd be flung back among us in the morning, covered in burns, injured, moaning, and would not always survive. I thought: 'Ha! If there were interrogations, he'd come and get me and I'd leave this room where I've always lived. He'd drag me along unknown corridors, and then something would happen!'

My mind worked incredibly fast: the boy was propelling me along with seeming dedication to his job, but, once we rounded the corner and were out of sight, he stopped, turned to me, smiled and said: 'Don't be afraid.' And then he took me in his arms and an immense sensation surged through me, an overwhelming eruption, an extraordinary burst of light exploding inside me. I couldn't breathe—and then I breathed again, because it was desperately brief.

After that, my mood changed. I no longer tried to persuade the women to tell me their secrets; I had my own. The eruption proved difficult to achieve. I had to tell myself stories that became increasingly long and complicated but, to my utter dismay, I never experienced that explosion twice in a row, whereas I wished it could have lasted for hours. I wanted to feel that sensation all the time, day and night, swaying deliciously, like the rare patches of grass on the plains caressed by the gentle breeze that blew for days at a time, but which I didn't see until much later.

I now devoted all my time to the task of producing the eruption. I had to invent exceptional circumstances where we found ourselves alone, or at least isolated in the midst of the others, face-to-face, and then, after much agony, I had the exquisite surprise of finding his arms around me. My imagination developed. I had to exercise rigorous discipline, because I couldn't dream up the same story twice: surprise was crucial, as I realised after trying several times to relive the exquisite gesture that had transported me, without feeling the slightest stirring. This was extremely difficult because I was simultaneously the inventor of the story, the narrator and the listener awaiting the shock of the unexpected. Thinking back, I'm amazed I managed to overcome so many obstacles! Imagine how fast my imagination had to work to prevent me from knowing what would happen so that I'd be caught unawares! The first time I imagined the interrogation, I'd never made up stories before, I didn't even know it was possible. I was completely swept along by it, marvelling both at such a new activity and at the story itself. Then I soon became adept at it, like a sort of narrative engineer. I could tell if it had begun badly or if it was heading towards an impasse, and could even go back to the beginning to change the course of events. I went so far as to create characters who reappeared regularly, who changed from one story to another, and who became old friends. I was delighted with them, and it is only now that I'm able to read books that I can see they were rather limited.

I needed to invent increasingly complicated stories: I think that deep down something inside me knew what I wanted from them and objected; I had to catch myself off guard. Sometimes I had to keep it up for several hours, to lull my inner audience into a false sense of security so that she'd be entranced by the pleasure of listening, enjoy the story and lower her defences. Then came the magic moment, the boy's gaze, his hand on my shoulder and the rapture that invaded my entire being. After that, I was able to sleep. Perhaps, in stopping the story, I was disappointing an inner listener who preferred the story to the turbulence, which is why she always spun it out and would happily have deprived me in order to prolong her own pleasure. Sometimes, halfway through, I'd try to argue with her: 'I'm tired, I want to go to sleep, let me get to the eruption, I'll carry on tomorrow.' But it was no use, she wouldn't let herself be fooled.

The women noticed that I'd changed. They observed me for a moment, saw me always sitting down, my knees tucked under, my chin resting on my folded arms, and I suppose I had a vacant stare. I was oblivious, because I wasn't bothered about them any more, and I was surprised when Annabel came to question me.

'What are you doing?'

'Thinking,' I replied.

That puzzled her. She stayed a little longer, waiting for me to say more, then went to convey my reply to the others. They argued for a while, and Annabel returned.

'What about?'

The full force of my anger returned.

'When I asked you what people do when they make love, you wouldn't tell me, and now you expect me to tell you what's going on inside my head! You keep your secrets, if it makes you happy, but don't expect me to tell you mine!'

She frowned and went back to the others. This time, the debate went on longer. I'd never seen them talk at such length and with such seriousness—usually they'd burst out laughing after ten minutes. Apparently I'd provoked something new in their minds. Another woman then stood up and came over to me. It was Dorothy, the eldest and most respected. Even I didn't hate her. She sat down and stared hard at me. Her presence annoyed me greatly because she was interrupting me at a crucial point in the story, which had been going on for a very long time: I was going to be locked up alone in a cell and had overheard a few words about the relief night guard who I had every reason to believe was the young man. How could I carry on in front of this old woman who was staring silently at me? At least I could try not to lose sight of the situation: I was alone, breathless and scared, and I could hear voices and the clink of weapons in the corridor. I didn't know what was going on and was frightened by the atmosphere of urgency and turmoil. I tried to suspend the scene in my mind while studying Dorothy who was studying me. I told myself that if the eruption didn't happen soon, I would have to make some sense out of the situation. But what on earth could I imagine that would feed back into the static world in which we lived, women locked up for so many years that they'd lost all notion of time?

'So, you've got a secret,' said Dorothy at long last.

I didn't reply, because it wasn't a real question. I could tell she was trying to faze me with her heavy stare and her silence. There was a time, before I'd found the inner world where I entertained myself, when I was still inquisitive and docile, when I'd have been intimidated. I'd have wondered what I'd done wrong to deserve this scrutiny, and I'd have feared the punishment. But now I knew I was beyond their reach: punishments were never more than being left out, excluded from futile, flighty conversations about nothing in particular, and that was all I wanted so that I could continue my secret pursuit in peace.

Since I didn't react, she frowned.

'I spoke to you. It is only polite to reply.'

'I have nothing to say. They told you I have secrets. You tell me they told you I did. Well, so what?'

'I want to hear them.'

I began to laugh, as much to my surprise as to anyone else's. I'd been used to respecting the women's wishes, especially those of the eldest who had the most authority, but everything had changed because I could no longer see any basis for that authority. I suddenly discovered that they had no power. We were all locked up in the same manner, without knowing why, watched over by jailers who, either out of contempt or because they were obeying orders, didn't speak to any of us. They never entered the cage. They were always in threes, except when they changed shift, and then we saw six at a time, but they didn't speak to one another. At mealtimes, one of the big double doors would open, a man would push a trolley along the gap between the cage and the wall, and another unlocked a little hatch through which he passed us the food. They wouldn't answer our questions and we had long since stopped asking them any. The old women were as helpless as the younger ones. They had seized some imaginary power, a power over nothing, a tacit agreement that created a meaningless hierarchy, because there were no privileges that they could grant or refuse. The fact is that we were on an absolutely equal footing.

I sat still for a few seconds, registering those familiar facts that suddenly became stunning revelations, and looking Dorothy squarely in the eyes.

'You want to hear my secrets,' I said, 'but all you can do is inform me of your wishes.'

I noted with interest the effect my words had on her: at first, when she saw that I was about to answer, she looked smug, she must have thought she'd won my obedience. Then she listened, and grasped the meaning of what I was saying, but she was so taken aback that she thought she hadn't understood.

'What do you mean?'

'Just think about it,' I said. 'I mean exactly what I said.'

'You haven't said anything!'

'I said I wouldn't tell you my secrets. You told me you wanted them. That's not telling me anything new, I was already aware of that. You think you only have to tell me you want to know for me to tell you.'

That was indeed what she thought.

'That is how things should be,' she insisted.

'Why?'

She was disconcerted. I saw she wasn't thinking about my question, she was so shocked that I could have asked it. She'd inherited a tradition to which I did not belong: when an older woman asks a younger woman to reply, the younger one does so. She'd never questioned that, but I, who had grown up in the bunker, had no reason to comply. After a few moments:

'What do you mean, "why"?'

'Why should I answer? Why do you think it goes without saying?'

Her gaze faltered. She tried to think, but she wasn't used to doing so. She looked confused and clutched at the first idea that came to her:

'You are insolent,' she said, relieved to find an explanation for the incomprehensible words I'd just uttered, certain that it would be enough to return to the habitual ways, to convention, to commonplaces.

'You're a fool,' I retorted, intoxicated by my new-found certainties. 'And this conversation is absurd. You think you have power but you're like the rest of us, reduced to receiving your share of food from enemy hands and with no means of punishing me if I rebel against you. Seeing as they forbid any authority other than theirs, you can neither beat me nor make me go without. Why should I obey you?'

This time it was clear that she wasn't taking in a word I was saying. I think she'd rather have gone deaf. She muttered, fidgeted a little, then signalled to two younger women to come and help her up, even though she could in fact manage unaided. She returned to her usual position at the other end of the cage. The women stared at her intently, without daring to ask any questions. She closed her eyes to give the impression she was thinking, and fell asleep.

'It's because she's old,' said the younger ones. 'An ordeal like that is too much for a woman of her age.'

They resumed their chatter and I returned to my story. I was back in the gloomy cell where I was in solitary confinement. I wasn't injured—the guards were always careful not to resort to blows. I was huddled in a corner, terrified, and my humiliating posture shocked me. Crouched and trembling—was that fitting for someone who'd just confronted one of the most respected women in the cage, looked her in the eyes and told her she was a fool? Dorothy had been lost for words. I felt a delicious shiver. That was, I think, my first intellectual pleasure. In my imaginary cell, I had to stand up, and now, I had to smile and defy them. It was hard to concentrate on the story, I'd enjoyed the minor battle I'd just waged, and I wanted to savour it, but it didn't cause the eruption because the young guard wasn't part of it, so I summoned my inner discipline to return to my private world.

If the women had had any sense, they'd have let matters rest there. It was still possible to pretend that nothing had happened and avoid an unequal battle. I'd realised that I was as strong as they were and that not confiding a secret, which is within everyone's grasp so long as there is no torture, immediately makes the secret seem infinitely precious. Their knowledge on the subject of love had seemed to me the ultimate object of desire when they'd refused to share it with me. Now, I scorned their pettiness, I told myself that in other times I'd have got what I wanted from the first boy who came along. In asking it of the women, I was granting them a prerogative that they'd never had, and it only underscored my ignorance. But now their curiosity was aroused, it was their turn to feel excluded and scorned. I'd found the eruption to console me: they remained disgruntled and powerless, sustained only by their gnawing exasperation. They began to watch me.

Watch? There were forty of us living in that big underground room where no one could hide from the others. At five-metre intervals, columns supported the vaulted ceiling and bars separated our living area from the walls, leaving a wide passage all around for the guards' relentless pacing up and down. No one ever escaped scrutiny and we were used to answering the call of nature in front of one another. At first—so they told me, my memories didn't go back that far—the women were most put out, they thought of forming a human wall to screen the woman relieving herself, but the guards prohibited it, because no woman was to be shielded from view. When I went to pass water, I found it perfectly natural to go and sit on the toilet seat and carry on my conversation—on the few occasions when I was engaged in conversation. The old women cursed furiously, complaining about the indignity of being reduced to the status of animals. If the only thing that differentiates us from animals is the fact that we hide to defecate, then being human rests on very little, I thought. I never argued with the women, in fact I already found them stupid, but I hadn't formulated it so clearly.

When I think back on it now, what a horrid little prig I was! I prided myself and revelled in having found a distraction that I thought was extraordinary. I felt as if I was being hounded by a mob, whereas we were all equally helpless prisoners. Isolated due to my young age and the constraints imposed on us, perhaps like the others I needed to create an illusion to enable me to cope with the misery. I have no idea. Now that I'm no longer able to go off hiking, I reflect a great deal, but, with no one to talk to, my thoughts soon start going round in circles. That's why it is interesting to write them down: I recognise them when they recur and I don't repeat them.

When Dorothy woke up and found the strength to relate our conversation to the others, she didn't tell them I'd called her a fool. But despite her efforts not to tarnish her image, she'd learned nothing of my secret and was unable to conceal the fact.

'A secret! A secret! What right does she have to keep a secret in a situation like this?'

Anthea, who was the brightest of the women, immediately grasped that it wasn't the actual content of the secret that mattered, but the fact that while living under the continual scrutiny of the other women, it was possible to claim to have a secret and be believed. This seemed too complicated for the women to understand and they dismissed Anthea with a gesture of annoyance, demanding that the secret be prised from me.

'We must force her. Make her tell us.'

'How will you do that?'

Carol, the stupidest and the most excitable, parked herself in front of me and in a threatening tone commanded me to speak.

'Or else!'

'Or else what?' I burst out laughing.

She made a violent gesture and it was obvious she was thinking of slapping me. It was so obvious that the guards, who never took their eyes off us, saw her at the same time as I did, and we heard the crack of the whip. We knew that they weren't aiming the blows at us, and that the whips only cracked in the air of the corridor around the cage, but the noise always frightened us and Carol jumped. None of the women remembered actually being hit, but Anthea told me about it later. It must have happened in the hazy period in the early days of our captivity for such a deep fear to have taken hold of us. No one ever disobeyed the whip, and the women sometimes described the bloody marks that the thongs made on bare skin, the searing pain that lasted for days. Several of the women bore long white scars. Terrified, Carol withdrew, and I gave her a sardonic smile. I was torn between the urge to scoff at her in silence, making the guards my allies, and wanting to explain her stupidity and helplessness to her, when Anthea intervened. She came over to Carol who was shaking with rage and fear, and motioned to her to move away.

'Come, it's pointless,' she said very softly.

A tremor ran through Carol's body, I thought she was going to fling herself into Anthea's arms, but we knew only too well that touching one another was prohibited, and she hung her head.

'Come,' repeated Anthea.

They went off side by side. I settled down again, my head on my knees, glad to be left in peace at last, but I was unable to immerse myself in my story again. That episode had made me jumpy. I was fidgety and couldn't regain my concentration. I got up and went over to the women peeling the vegetables and offered to help. But I was clumsy and that annoyed them.

'Oh, go away and play!' said one of them.

'Who with?'

I was the youngest, the only one who'd still been a child when we were locked up. The women had always believed I'd ended up among them by mistake, that in the chaos I'd been sent to the wrong side and no one had noticed. Once the cages were locked, they would probably never reopen. Sometimes, the women said that the keys must be lost, and that even if the guards wanted to, they wouldn't be able to release us. I think it was a joke, but I'd forgotten about it until now, and it was too late to check.

Alice, the woman who'd dismissed me, seemed embarrassed. She looked at me sadly, perhaps she felt sorry for me and disapproved of the women who were determined to wrest my secret from me.

'It's true, poor thing. You're all alone.' She looked sympathetic, and that calmed me down a little. The women weren't often kind to me. I suppose that at that time they resented my being there alive while they had no idea what had happened to their own daughters. The appalling disaster that had befallen us probably explained their attitude: none of them ever bothered about me or made the slightest attempt to comfort me. But perhaps that wasn't possible? My own mother wasn't with us and we had no notion what had become of the others. We assumed they were probably all dead. I have raked through my memories of that time, I thought I saw them swaying and groaning, crying and shivering with terror. None of them looked at me and I hated them. I thought it was unfair, and then I understood that, alone and terrified, anger was my only weapon against the horror.

I moved away from Alice and went and sat down again, my legs tucked under me, but I was unable to pick up the thread of my reverie. I was bored. For lack of any other distraction, I began observing them. That day, we'd been given leeks and coarsely cut mutton. As they scrubbed the vegetables, the women argued noisily over how they were going to cook them. I never paid much attention to what I ate, which in my view was neither good nor bad, unless I was still hungry when my plate was empty, which was rare because I had little appetite. Listening to their chatter, I was amazed—anyone would think they had the choice between several recipes and a variety of seasonings, whereas in fact they only had three large pots and water. There was never any option but to boil the vegetables. We'd eat them for lunch and the stock would serve as soup in the evening. Sometimes, extra food was brought in the afternoon, a few kilos of pasta, or, very occasionally, potatoes—nothing that gave much scope for imagination. This was probably their way of telling one another stories; they did what they could. They said—and I had heard it hundreds of times, but without taking any notice—that the stock tasted different depending on whether you put the meat in first or the vegetables, that you could also cook the ingredients separately, shred the leek leaves, or reduce the stock to make it tastier. They bustled around chatting. This was the first time I'd listened closely, and I was surprised at how much they had to say, the passion with which they repeated the same thing in ten different ways so as to avoid accepting that they'd had absolutely nothing to say to one another for ages. But human beings need to speak, otherwise they lose their humanity, as I've realised these past few years. And gradually, I began to feel sorry for those women determined to carry on living, pretending they were active and making decisions in the prison where they were locked up for ever, from which death was the only release—but would they remove the bodies?—and where they couldn't even kill one another.

I suddenly found myself contemplating our situation. Until that moment, I'd simply endured it without thinking about it, as if it were a natural state. Do we wonder why we're sleepy at night, or hungry when we wake up? I knew, as did the others, that suicide was one of the things that was prohibited. At first, some of the more desperate or more active women had tried the knife or the rope, and that showed how closely the guards were watching us, because they immediately heard the crack of the whip. The guards were excellent marksmen, reaching their target from a distance, slashing the belts the women were planning to use as ropes, or jerking the crudely sharpened knife from the hands that held it. They wanted to ensure we stayed alive, which made the women believe that they wanted to use us in some way, that there were plans. They imagined all sorts of things, but nothing ever happened. We were fed, not over-generously, which caused those who were too fat to lose weight, and we didn't really lack for anything. We had to cook our meals in huge pots and to hand back the two blunt knives when the vegetables were peeled. Occasionally, we were given a few lengths of fabric to make clothes. They were crudely fashioned since we had no scissors and we had to tear the fabric very carefully. I wrote a moment ago that nothing ever happened, but that's not exactly true: the arrival of the pieces of material created great excitement. We knew which dresses were worn-out beyond repair, and which ones could still be salvaged, and we'd embark on complicated calculations to enable us to make the best use of the new cotton. We had to take into account the quantity of thread that came with it; sometimes there were remnants of fabric but we had nothing with which to sew them together. One day, Dorothy came up with the idea of using hair as thread. She recalled how, a very long time ago, hair had been used for embroidery. Anna and Laura had the longest hair, which we used for our first attempts. These were unsuccessful because the hairs snapped. Then someone suggested plaiting several hairs and we achieved a certain degree of success: the stitches didn't hold for long, but there was plenty more hair to redo them.

The guards didn't give us sanitary towels or toilet paper, which the women complained about a great deal. I had no recollection of ever using either, so I managed very well with running water, which was in plentiful supply, and, since I didn't have periods, I didn't have the worry of what to do about the blood. The women collected the tiniest scraps of material and used them for their periods, then rinsed them thoroughly in the water, because we received very little soap, which was black and runny, and we kept it for washing our bodies.

This almost total lack of physical activity would have made us weak, but we forced ourselves to do exercises every day, which was the most boring thing in the world, but even I put up with it because I realised it was necessary. Once or twice a woman was ill: a thermometer was included in the supplies and the whip made it clear that she was to take her temperature. Medicine would arrive if she was feverish. We seem to have been in rather good health. What with the food and the continuous lighting and heating, we must have been costing someone or something a lot of money, but we didn't know why they were going to so much trouble. In their previous lives, the women had worked, borne children and made love. All I knew was that these things were greatly valued. What use were we here?

I was taken aback by my thoughts. Suddenly, the secret that was being denied me and the one I didn't want to share seemed to be of little worth compared with that of the guards: what were we doing here, and why were we being kept alive?

I went over to Anthea who had always been the least hostile towards me. She smiled at me.

'Well, have you come to tell me your secret?'

I gave an irritable shrug.

'Don't be as stupid as the others,' I said. 'Look at them. They're pretending, they behave as though they still have some control over their lives and make momentous decisions about which vegetable to cook first. What are we doing here?'

Anthea looked wary. 'What do you mean?'

'We can't talk about that either! You spend your time kidding yourself that you know things, and you're using me, who doesn't know a thing, to convince yourself of your superiority! No one has any idea why we are being so carefully guarded and you're afraid to think about it.'

'Don't always talk about us as a group.'

'Well, let's talk about you. Answer me with your own thoughts. If you have any.'

We're not allowed to hit one another, but if we talk calmly and don't allow our expressions to betray anger, we can exchange cutting words.

I WHO HAVE NEVER KNOWN MEN

'What's the use of talking about it? It won't make any difference.'

'There you go again with your stupidity! As if talking only served to make things happen. Talking is existing. Look: they know that, they talk for hours on end about nothing.'

'But will talking teach us anything about what we're doing here? You have no more idea than I or any of the rest of us do.'

'True, but I'll know what you think, you'll know what I think, and perhaps that will spark off a new idea, and then we'll feel as if we're behaving like human beings rather than robots.'

She put down the piece of fabric she was sewing with plaited hairs and folded her hands on her knees.

'Is that what you're doing, when you sit alone with your eyes closed, thinking about us?'

'I do as I please. Don't try and force my secret out of me, I'm not some featherbrain who can be tricked so easily.'

She laughed.

'You'd have been very bright! You'd have had a great future, you would!'

'We have no future any more. All we can do is entertain ourselves by conversing.'

'You make fun of the discussion over the vegetables, and yet what you suggest is just as pointless.'

I began to laugh. It was most enjoyable having someone as intelligent as myself to talk to.

'I find the subject more interesting. Do we know why they locked us up?'

'No.'

'Or where the others are?'

'If there is a reason, we don't know what it is. Since we're here, and we're being kept alive, we think there must be others alive somewhere, but there's no evidence, and that's just as well. No one has the slightest idea what's behind all this. There isn't the slightest clue. They rounded up the adults—you're almost certainly here by accident. At first—well, not really at first, because there's a period that remains hazy in everybody's minds—but after that, from the time when our memories became clearer, we know we used to think all the time. They could have killed you—but they don't kill—or taken you away, sent you elsewhere, if there are other prisons like this one, but then your arrival would have brought news, and the one thing we are certain of is that they don't want us to know anything. We came to the conclusion that they left you here because any decision can be analysed, and that their lack of decision indicated the only thing they wanted us to know, which is that we must know nothing.'

Never had any of the women spoken to me at such length. I sensed that she'd passed on to me everything she knew, and I experienced a mild light-headedness which was rather pleasant. It reminded me vaguely of the eruption and I promised myself I'd see if I could work it into one of my stories.

'Can you tell me anything else?'

'Nothing.'

She sighed and took up her needlework, inspecting it mechanically.

'And we'll never be any the wiser. We will die, one by one, as age gets the better of us. Dorothy will probably be the first, she has a bad heart. She looks over seventy. I don't think I'm forty yet; with no seasons, we can't keep track of time. You will be the last.'

She stared at me for ages without saying a word. Since I had greatly exercised my imagination of late, I could guess her thoughts: one day, I would be alone in the huge grey room. In the morning, a guard would pass me my food, which I'd cook on the hotplate, and I'd eat, sleep and die alone, without having understood our fate or why it had been inflicted on us. I was scared stiff.

'Is there nothing we can do?'

'There's not one of us who hasn't thought of killing herself, but they're too quick. You mustn't try and hang yourself: twist a piece of fabric into a rope and the minute you start tying it to the bars, they'll be there. Mary, who's sitting over there talking to Dorothy, tried to starve herself to death: they chased her with the whip and harassed her until she gave up. You know the knives they give us: they're completely blunt. They're just about good enough for scraping carrots, and we're not allowed to try and sharpen them. Once, a long time ago, Alice, one of the most desperate women, persuaded another woman to strangle her. It happened at night, after they'd turned the lights down. We thought the guards were pacing up and down automatically, deceived by our stillness: but they watch us so closely all the time, that they realised what was happening and the whips cracked.'

'They never touch us.'

'At one time they did, there were wounds that were very slow to heal. We don't know why they stopped. There's no point rebelling. We must just wait until we die.'

She resumed her sewing. She was piecing together the least worn parts of a dress to make something or other. When I think back on it, I tell myself the lengths of fabric were almost excessive: it was hot in the bunker and we could have lived without clothes. I picture the two latrines in the centre of the room. Since there were forty of us, there was nearly always a woman sitting there doing her business, and I found it hard to believe that they allowed us to cover ourselves to satisfy our modesty. I watched Anthea and it occurred to me that seeing as I would be the last, I'd better learn to sew. Unless the women who died left me their clothing, and those hand-me-downs would last me until the end.

I was sad. I'd always hated my cellmates because of their indifference to me and I'd never spared a thought for them. On our arrival here, they'd been overwhelmed by their fear and despair, and I'd remained isolated, a terrified little girl surrounded by weeping women. In dying, they'd be abandoning me once more. Anger welled up inside me. So they had thought about our situation, they'd been wondering about it for a long time, and they'd always excluded me from their discussions. Anthea was the first to take the trouble to talk to me. I'd found our conversation interesting and had been determined to listen to her, to think, and forget that for years she'd ignored me just as the others had.

'Why are you talking to me today?'

She looked taken aback.

'But you're the one who came to speak to me,' she said. 'You're always on your own, as if you don't want to join in with us.'

I was about to tell her that they always stopped talking when I drew near, but suddenly I felt terribly tired. Perhaps I was unused to conversing at such length. She saw me yawn.

'They'll be turning the lights down soon. Let's get ready for bed. We'll speak more tomorrow.'

Of course I was unable to sleep. I wanted to carry on with the story that Annabel had interrupted at the point when I was in a cell waiting for the young guard to appear, but I couldn't concentrate. Usually, when I told myself a story, I became completely impervious to what was going on around me, but that evening, the comings and goings of the women arranging mattresses, whispering and the gradual descent of silence all disrupted my train of thought. I reflected on the years, the grief, those lost husbands, the children they'd never seen again, and wondered about my own mother, since I must have had a mother. I couldn't remember her. I only knew that there must have been someone I called mummy, and who wasn't in the prison. Was she dead? I went over the little I'd heard about the disaster, which boiled down to a few words: screams, the scramble, night and a growing terror. They thought they must have fainted, perhaps several times, and that everything had happened very quickly. On reflection I concluded that this explanation was not enough. There were forty of us who had nothing in common, whereas before each woman had had a family, parents, brothers, sisters, friends: only a meticulous selection could have only brought together strangers. This was confirmed by Anthea the next day.

'Just think what a huge job that must have been: they made sure that none of us knew any of the others. They took us from all four corners of the country, and even from several countries, checking that fate had not thrown together two cousins or friends separated by circumstances.'

'Why? What are they looking for?'

'We nearly drove ourselves mad asking that same question. You were too young, you couldn't understand, and you'd curl up into a ball on the ground, you wouldn't answer when we spoke to you.'

'I don't remember that.'

'We didn't think you'd get over it. As we weren't allowed to touch one another, nobody could pick you up and cuddle you or try and comfort you, or even make you eat. We thought you were going to die, but, very slowly, you began to move again. You sidled up to the food at mealtimes and swallowed a few mouthfuls. Then, naturally, we got into the habit of never going over our few memories in front of you, we thought it would be bad for you. And, gradually, we wearied of talking about them among ourselves. It didn't help. Asking the same questions, in the same way, for years—you eventually tire of it.'

'And you live like this, with your vegetables, with no prospects?'

'Only death,' she snapped. 'We can't commit suicide, but we will still die. We just have to wait.'

I'd never thought about our situation so clearly. In my stories, there were always things happening: in my life, nothing would ever happen. I realised that she was right and that the secrets of love were none of my business. Perhaps they'd pretended to know more than me because they knew nothing of the essential. I suspected that the men hadn't complied like the women: but since I would never encounter a man, what did this difference matter? It was the girls in another era who had to be prepared for their wedding night, I told myself.

That day seemed very short, and I put that down to the intensity of my thinking. When the lights were dimmed, we had to lay out the forty mattresses on which we slept. There wasn't enough room, they were almost touching, and every morning we piled them up three or four high so we could move around and sit on them. I stretched out and tried to pick up the thread of my story, but was unable to, my mind was blank and there was an overwhelming feeling of grief in my breast.

'Close your eyes,' my neighbour said. 'Don't let them see you're not asleep.'

It was Frances, one of the younger women, one of those who'd never laughed at me.

'Why?'

'Don't you notice anything? Anyone would think you'd just arrived from another planet. They won't allow us not to sleep.

If they see your eyes open they call you over to the bars and make you take a pill.'

'Call? But they never talk to us!'

'Oh yes they do! With their whips!'

I understood what she meant. It was very rare for a woman to disobey: but when it happened, the whip cracked beside her, until she did as she was told. They were merciless, and handled their whips with the utmost precision: they could crack it twenty times in a row by someone's ear, and if the woman it was intended for resisted, there was always another who gave in. When Alice, whom they'd forced to eat, tried to strangle herself with her dress twisted into a rope, Claudia had relented and rushed to undo the knot and halt the appalling threat of death, always promised, never given. I closed my eyes.

'What's stopping you from getting to sleep?' asked Frances.

'How do you get to sleep?'

She didn't answer. I was choked by sobs. 'Are we allowed to cry? Without pills?'

'No—you'd better control yourself.'

Then, something strange happened inside me, I wanted to feel her arms around me and it was so sudden, so unexpected, that I was overcome. I threw myself into her arms before I realised what I was doing.

'Stop!' she whispered, horrified.

And the whip cracked above my head. I recoiled, terrified. This was the first time it had been aimed at me. I still shudder to think of it. I curled up, panting as if I'd been running.

Running? I had never run!

I knew very well that we weren't permitted to touch one another and, since I'd never known any different, I took it for granted. The rush of feeling I'd just experienced created confused notions in me: holding hands, walking with arms around each other, holding each other—those words were part of my vocabulary, they described gestures I had never made. A walk? I remembered maybe lawns, or seasons, because those words had a very distant ring, a faint echo that quickly died away. I knew the flaking grey walls, the bars at fifteen-centimetre intervals, the guards pacing regularly up and down around the perimeter of the room.

'What do they want of us?' I asked again. She shrugged.

'All we know is what they don't want.'

She looked away and it was plain that the conversation was at an end. Anthea was the first woman to talk to me for any length of time, perhaps she would be the only one?

I concentrated on keeping my eyes closed, in the hope that eventually I'd fall asleep. For the first time, I understood that I was living at the very heart of despair. I had insulated myself from it, believing that it was out of bitterness, but suddenly I realised it was out of caution, and that all these women who lived without knowing the meaning of their existence were mad. Whether it was their fault or not, they'd gone mad by force of circumstance, they'd lost their reason because nothing in their lives made sense any more.

I didn't know how old I was. Since I didn't have periods and I had virtually no breasts, some of the women thought I wasn't yet fourteen, barely thirteen, but Anthea, who was more logical than the others, thought that I must be around fifteen or sixteen.

'We don't know how long we've been here. Looking at your height, you're no longer a child, and some of us stopped menstruating a long time ago. Anna's young, she doesn't have any wrinkles, neither do I, so they say. It isn't the menopause that has withered us, it's despair.'

'So men were very important?'

She nodded.

'Men mean you are alive, child. What are we, without a future, without children? The last links in a broken chain.'

'So life gave such great pleasure?'

'You have so little idea what it meant to have a destiny that you can't understand what it means to be deprived as we are. Look at the way we live: we know we have to behave as if it's morning, because they make the lights brighter, then they pass us food and, at a given time, the lights are dimmed. We're not even certain they make us live according to a twenty-four-hour pattern. How would we measure time? They've reduced us to utter helplessness.'

Her tone was harsh and she stared straight ahead. Once again, I felt like crying. I curled up into a ball.

'What's the matter?'

All of a sudden, her voice was so gentle, so lilting, that I trembled as if being caressed. At least, I suppose it could be described thus: something exquisite coursed through me, so delicious that it frightened me. I curled up even tighter.

'I don't want to talk any more,' I told her. 'I was happier when I hadn't understood anything, when I hated you all because you kept your secrets. You don't have any. You have nothing, and there is nothing to be had.'

'What secrets did you think we had?'

I no longer felt humiliated by my ignorance, because I'd touched on a knowledge that was too painful to bear.

'How you make love, with what, what happens, all that. There they are, telling each other stories from the past, making allusions and bursting out laughing, and clamming up when I approach. I thought that was what was important, but it's all pointless.'

'Poor child,' she said, so tenderly and so sadly that I burst into tears.

They probably tolerated crying, as long as we sobbed quietly and didn't cause a stir; the whip didn't crack.

Some food arrived and there was a bit of a flurry. When we felt hungry for the second time since the morning, we said it was the evening. We cooked whatever there was, we ate, and shortly afterwards the lights dimmed. The women said that, before the disaster, people used to eat three times a day, in the morning, at noon and in the evening, but we only felt hungry twice during each waking period and we were not sure that we were living according to the same clock as before. It was one of the arguments that came up time and time again, but kept going round in circles because nothing ever changed. Was it that we needed less food since we didn't work, and two meals a day were sufficient? Had our bodies forgotten old habits to the extent that we could sleep every eight or ten hours? But, did we know how long we slept for? Perhaps they kept us awake for eight hours and only gave us nights of four hours, or six? The guards were relieved at intervals that didn't correspond to those of our lives—sometimes in the middle of the day, sometimes at night, or twice in one day. I was watching them, mustering the little knowledge I had, when I became aware that the young guard with blue eyes must have been away: suddenly, I saw him, pacing up and down the length of the cage, and I realised that I hadn't thought about him or told myself any stories for several days. He still looked just as handsome.

I went to fetch my plate of food and sat down next to Anthea.

'Handsome, beautiful—I suppose they're words from before, from when things happened?' I asked her.

She gazed at me for a while, then looked away.

'I was beautiful,' she said. 'I don't know if I still am, I'd need a mirror. My hair has gone grey, but that doesn't mean I'm old, the women in my family go grey early. My memories are muddled, I think I was twenty-eight the year they locked us up. At first, I still took the trouble to do my hair, and I was very upset about losing my brushes.'

She spoke in a half-whisper, as if to herself, but I knew she was talking to me.

'And then my dress wore out. It was a pretty summer frock, very fashionable, with flounces, in that delicate fabric that doesn't last very long. I was one of the first to wear these sort of tunics we make. Now, there are no dresses from before left, not even any scraps, they're all worn out down to the last thread. You can't imagine what they were like.'

'Being beautiful, was that for the men?'

I was almost sure it was, but I sometimes heard the women say otherwise.

'Yes. Some women say that it is for ourselves. What on earth can we do with it? I could have loved myself whether I was hunchbacked or lame, but to be loved by others, you had to be beautiful.'

'Am I beautiful?'

I saw her smile, but her smile was heart-rending.

'Yes,' she said. 'Yes. You'd probably have been one of the prettiest girls because you wouldn't have had that sulky, angry expression. You'd have laughed, you'd have provoked the boys.'

'Sometimes I provoke the young guard,' I burst out.

This I had just understood.

When I told myself stories, I always went to sit close to the bars, on the side where he paced up and down. He walked slowly, keeping a close watch on what was going on in the cage, as he always did. Crouching down, facing him, I kept still, following him with my eyes. I watched him, and because he saw everything, he couldn't have been unaware that I was watching him. Just a girl, sitting there, wearing her shapeless tunic. My hair was long and I kept it tied back at the nape of my neck; other than that, I have no idea what I looked like. I didn't even know what colour my eyes were until Anthea told me, later, and I had no idea what that meant, to be one of the prettiest girls. It didn't occur to me that none of the women was beautiful: they were clean, we kept the little soap we were given for washing our bodies and our hair, which was always clean. Most of us had long hair, because we had nothing to cut it with. Nor did we have anything for cutting our nails, which were always breaking when they were too long, and we looked sad, except when there were outbursts of nervous giggles. I don't know what expression I wore when I looked at the guard: I was totally preoccupied, I was all eyes. He never looked at me: I was sure he knew I was staring at him continually and that it made him feel awkward.

'I'd like to make him lose his composure.'

'Whatever for?' asked Anthea, in surprise.

'I don't know. To have power over him. They have the whip and they make us do what they want, which is almost nothing. They forbid everything. I'd like him to be upset, worried, afraid, unable to react. We've never been forbidden to sit and stare.'

'Perhaps they'll forbid it. They forbid what they like.'

'Then they'd be acknowledging my existence. If you do something that is forbidden, it is the action that is the target. If you do something that isn't forbidden, and they intervene, then it's not the activity that's attracting attention, it's you yourself.'

She was the brightest of the women, but I'd grasped something that she hadn't thought of, so I was at least as clever as she was! A delicious thrill ran through me and I smiled at her.

'They feed forty women, they keep us warm and give us fabric to make clothes. For them, we have no names, they treat us as if there is no difference between one woman and another. But I'm me. I'm not a fortieth of the herd, one cow among the others. I'm going to stare at him until he's embarrassed.'

I marvelled at my own audacity. For years, we'd been here, reduced to utter helplessness, deposed, deprived even of instruments with which to kill ourselves, defecating under the full glare of the lights, in front of the others, in front of them: and I wanted to embarrass a guard and thought I had found the way to do it.

'Don't breathe a word to anyone. I don't want the women to know what's going on. They would change their attitude, they wouldn't be able to help it, and what I am doing would lose all its power.'

'Suppose we all started staring at them—wouldn't they be even more embarrassed?'

'They would no longer be embarrassed at all.'

These thoughts came to me with dazzling certainty and I felt absolutely sure of them. Where did they come from? I still have no idea, I only know that I derived enormous pleasure from what was going on in my mind.

'Something that everybody does becomes meaningless. It's just a habit, a custom, nobody knows when it started, they just repeat it mechanically. If I want to annoy him, I must be the only one to stare at him.'

Anthea pondered. I'm not sure she completely understood me; I was driven by an unquestionable authority and nothing was going to stop me.

'I don't know what all this may lead to,' I told her, 'but that's what's so exciting: in our absurd existence, I've invented something unexpected.'

She gently nodded her head.

'Go on,' she said. 'And I shall carry on thinking about it.'

And I resumed my position, sitting cross-legged, my eyes riveted on the young guard.

Was he really handsome or did I only find him handsome because he was the only man who wasn't old? I, who knew so little, and who couldn't remember the world, did recognise the signs of age. I'd seen hair turn grey, and then white, speckles appear, baldness threaten the heads of the oldest women, wrinkles, dry skin, folds, weakening tendons, stooped backs. The guard had clear skin, his step was supple as I knew mine was, despite the little space there was for me to test it; he was upright and young like me. I found that strange: weren't there enough old men left? Maybe they were all dead? Or did they not know what to do with the young men? They couldn't think of any more tasks to set them and so they sent them to pace up and down between the bars and the wall? There hadn't been any young guards before, I said to myself, and my heart began to race. How long had he been there? I had the feeling that I hadn't noticed him straight away, I hadn't counted the days, I didn't know when I'd started making up stories because I had no reference points. Unless I was mistaken, if his presence was recent, then, for the first time in years, something had changed. Beyond the walls, in that outside world which was totally concealed from us except for the food we ate and the fabric they gave us, things had happened and those events affected us. The guards had always been so old that we didn't notice them age. I'd been a little girl when I arrived, now I was a woman, a virgin for ever, but an adult despite my underdeveloped breasts and my aborted puberty: I'd grown, my body had recorded the passage of time. The old women didn't change any more than the old guards, their hair had turned white, but it happened so slowly that it was hardly noticeable. I'd been their clock: watching me, the women watched their own time tick by. Maybe that was why they didn't like me, perhaps the mere fact of my existence made them cry. The young guard wasn't a child when he arrived, he was tall, with thick hair, and there were no lines on his face. When he showed the first signs of withering, then I would feel my own skin to see whether I was getting older. He too would be a clock, we would grow old at the same speed. I could watch him and judge how much time I had left from the springiness of his step.

So, there had been a change. Somewhere, a decision had been taken which affected us, the impact of which we could assess: one of the old men had disappeared—perhaps he'd died—and had been replaced. Had this escaped the notice of those who governed our lives, were they not concerned about giving us a piece of information, or had they relaxed their vigilance?

I didn't take my eyes off the guards. They always went in threes, pacing up and down the corridor. They were silent. When they passed one another, their eyes didn't meet but I had the impression that they watched each other as closely as they watched us. The authorities must have been afraid that they'd disobey orders, or that they'd speak to us. Once again, I had a sudden insight, I understood why they had to be in threes: it prevented any complicity. They weren't permitted to have private conversations, which might have conveyed something to us; they had to maintain the role of suspicious jailers all the time.

The two men on duty with the young guard had been there for ages. During the early years, the women had tried to talk to the guards, to make demands or move them to pity, but nothing could break down their cruel indifference. Then, they gave up and behaved as if they couldn't see the guards, as if they'd banished their presence from their minds—or as if they themselves were bars that the women had become so used to that they no longer bumped into them. Nobody imagined that they felt in the least humiliated, but the prisoners' pride was preserved intact. They no longer complained to the guards or took their imperturbability as an insult. And that made the gaze of this girl, sitting absolutely still, all the more powerful.

I'd stopped telling myself stories: watching the guard, I was creating one. I needed patience, I had nothing else to give. I don't know how many waking periods I spent in this way. I thought a lot, and it occurred to me that we should stop speaking in terms of day and night, but of waking and sleeping periods. My certainty grew stronger: we were not living according to a twenty-four-hour cycle. When the lights were turned down, no one was tired: the women said it was because they had nothing to do. Perhaps they were right, but I didn't know what it was like to work. My conviction came from continually watching the young guard. The relief guards didn't come when we awoke, at mealtimes, when we went to bed or when we were moving around, but in between, at irregular intervals. The main door would open a fraction, the three men pacing up and down around the cage would converge, and sometimes they'd all leave the room as the next shift entered; at other times, only one or two were replaced. Was there any connection between their timetable and ours? How could I measure the passage of time? The only indicators I had were my body rhythms.

Anthea taught me that the heart always beats at the same rate, between seventy and seventy-four times a minute in a healthy person.

I began to count.

I had learned very little. Thirty, forty, fifty, seventy, eighty, I had to sort out the tens in my mind, but then I realised I didn't know my tables and I barely knew how to do division. If, between the time when they turned the lights full on and the time when the guards changed shift, when the young guard came on duty, my heart had beaten seven thousand, two hundred times, that would have made a hundred minutes. It was just a question of multiplying Anthea's seventy-two by a hundred, but what I had was three thousand, two hundred and twenty, or five thousand and twelve! I was incapable of performing the necessary operations. It was all very well concentrating and counting, but I couldn't make use of the figures I obtained.

'Can you teach me to do sums?' I asked Anthea.

'Without pencil and paper?'

She explained:

'We are not as heartless as you think, and we have discussed your education a great deal. Teach you to read? With what, and to read what? Counting was possible up to a point, but only for mental calculations and we weren't able to show you arithmetical operations. You wouldn't know how to read a number. Helen and Isabel taught you your tables, but you must have forgotten because you never used them. Besides, when you realised that it wasn't a game, you refused, it made you cross. We couldn't force you and we couldn't punish you, because of the guards. We couldn't make you want to learn things you thought were pointless, and, in the end, we didn't really see the need. Eight eights, and what then? What do you find sixty-four of here? Was there any point teaching you anything?'

I knew what reading was, but I'd never seen anything written. At most, I had understood the idea of letters, of their configuration, of words. The women had spoken of books and of poets.

'If ever we get out, I'll be stupid.'

'If ever …'

She stared at me and I sensed that images were going through her mind, of which I had no idea. Of course, I must have seen the sun, the trees, days and nights, but I had no recollection whatsoever. Although I could guess what filled Anthea's inner gaze, I couldn't picture those things.

'I'm afraid there's no chance of that, you poor child,' she said after a while. 'But it's true that if that were to happen, you'd be able to criticise us for having been very poor teachers, and we'd delight in your criticism.'

I looked at the women: they'd just been given the vegetables, and were bustling about as usual, trying to find a new way of cooking cabbage and carrots when all they had was water and salt. They didn't seem so stupid, because I understood that, having nothing in their lives, they took the little that came and made the best use of it, exploiting the slightest event to nourish their starving spirits.

'Yesterday, between the time when the lights came full on and when the young guard arrived, in other words when they changed shift, my heart produced three thousand, two hundred and twenty beats, and today, five thousand and twelve. How long is that?'

I saw her gasp.

'What? Did you count them?'

'It could help measure time.'

The young guard paced slowly up and down the length of the cage, the other two followed a few steps behind him. They never moved away from one another, they never walked side by side. While talking to Anthea, I kept my eyes on my prey: he never once looked in my direction.

'If you counted, the least I can do is try and work it out,' she said. 'It's such a long time since I did that! But do I know how fast your heart beats?'

'You told me what a normal rate was.'

'Yes, but there are variations from one person to another, and how do I know whether your heart beats at a normal rate? I can't even take your pulse since we're not allowed to touch.'

'I can take it, I already have. I'll say "tick-tock" at each beat. Compare that with your own heart, it'll give us something to start from.'

My rate was slower than hers.

'You're younger. You are probably closer to the average than I am; my heart used to beat quite fast. How can we tell?'

'What does it matter if the unit isn't precise? The main thing is to have a unit. Take seventy-two.'

'No. Given that we can't be sure anyway, I'll divide by seventy. It's easier, and even then, I'm not sure I won't get in a muddle.'

She fell silent, her eyes glazed over and she began to mumble. I listened to her without taking my eyes off the guard.

'Three thousand, two hundred and twenty divided by seventy makes forty-six. At least, I think it does. I'm amazed it goes exactly. I'm going to start again.'

One of the old guards stared at me intently for two or three seconds.

'Yes, it's definitely forty-six. I'll try five thousand and twelve.'

The guards had the time to complete their round before she finished.

'Seventy-one or seventy-two, there are fractions.'

'So that's either forty-six minutes after we get up, or seventy-one or seventy-two?'

'Forty-six minutes, or one hour and eleven or twelve minutes.'

She was thrilled.

'How odd! What connection can there be between forty-six minutes and one hour twelve?'

I was lost.

'We used to work seven or eight hours a day, depending on what our job was,' she explained. 'We'd begin at the same time every day, or people worked shifts, to ensure continuity. But we never had variations of twenty-five or twenty-six minutes from one day to the next. Does that mean something?'

She was alluding to a way of life that I knew nothing about, and I could only listen to her.

'Carry on counting. Count the times tomorrow.'

Tomorrow? But was it tomorrow in the old sense of the word?

This first achievement made me ambitious. I told myself that heartbeats were not the only rhythms, and I started listening to my body. I knew that menstruation occurred every twenty-eight days and I was saddened that I didn't possess that indicator, but I observed the variations in my appetite. Sometimes, I was very hungry when I woke up, and it felt like a long time until the meal was ready. We'd got it into our heads that they gave us food at specific times, but I saw that this was mistaken. Between the two meals, sometimes three hours went by, sometimes five. When I'd counted about ten times, it seemed that the young guard arrived at different times. I won't list the figures I obtained—although I remember them perfectly, for they are the birth dates of my thoughts. Anthea found them so odd that she wondered whether the times weren't completely random. But the young guard almost never stayed longer than six hours, according to my heart. When he appeared, he looked fresh and rested—from watching him, I had come to know him well—but at the end of his shift, he showed little signs of fatigue. His step maintained its elasticity, he held his head high: I couldn't say precisely what it was that suggested weariness. Was he a little paler? His gaze less penetrating? Were his movements just a fraction slower? The relief guard always came on duty at times that were separate from our meal and sleep times. I found that strange.

'This gives us a clue,' I told Anthea. 'Their time is not the same as ours. We and the guards live together, in fact: wouldn't it be natural for us to follow the same patterns?'

I could see that she hadn't grasped my reasoning.

'When one of the guards doesn't appear for seven or eight hours, presumably it's because he's gone off to sleep. But those periods are never the same as our sleep times. I shall have to keep watch, to make a mental note of their absences.'

Anthea looked puzzled, then frowned and nodded.

'What can two different time patterns mean?'

'You're the one who's known the real world. I can't make anything of it.'

She told me that she was unable to make any sense of it either. She couldn't connect the two things and she felt it was time to take the other women into our confidence.

'I can't think any more. It's all too complicated, I can't absorb all the facts. We must share what we've discovered, and ask the others what they think.'

Obviously, I was none too pleased, but I realised that Anthea was out of her depth and I gave her my permission. She went about it through discreet little chats: she took one or two women to one side, warned them that she was about to tell them something astonishing, and asked them to keep their expressions blank so as not to alert the guards. The idea of being astonished by the life we led already caused a stir, and Anthea quickly became adept at calming them down. During the early years, they'd learned to control themselves, then, with the absurd monotony of the days, they'd no longer had anything to control. The announcement of something new sent them into a tizzy. At first, the novelty itself was less of a shock than the fact of its existence. They said: 'It's not possible!' and then they faltered. Anthea invented techniques. She began by saying:

'Stay calm. Carry on with what you were doing'—peeling a vegetable, finishing off some sewing, plaiting their hair, there were so few things to do—'without altering your speed. To do that, you need to be aware of your speed, of your movements.' On hearing this, the women were of course intrigued, but only moderately. Because we lived under surveillance, the idea of remaining impassive was quickly understood, and they followed Anthea's orders without difficulty. The word got around that something extraordinary was happening and, above all, that they must not give anything away. It seemed to me that if there was a little buzz of excitement, it was discreet enough to escape the guards' attention. The women had chattered happily about everything when there was nothing to talk about, and there didn't appear to be any change. They took stock of what they knew about the world before, and realised that they'd forgotten a lot. Most of them were not very well educated, and had lived quietly taking care of their homes, their children, the shopping and housework. I don't think they had much to forget. They started to cogitate; their minds were numbed and they found it hard.

They couldn't think of anything.

Meanwhile, I carried on counting. Gradually, I managed to count automatically, while I was chatting or eating, and soon, in my sleep. I woke up with a number in my mind: at first, it seemed improbable. I was dubious, then convinced. Anthea told me I'd developed an aptitude which was perhaps not as extraordinary as all that; it was simply that no one had ever needed it before.

I counted my heartbeats one by one, and I soon found myself faced with huge numbers that defied mental calculations. At seventy-two beats a minute, an hour was equal to more than four thousand, two hundred, and by the end of the day I had reached over fifty thousand. It was no longer manage-able. So I found a different technique: I counted seventy-two then I mentally chalked up one. I started again and chalked up two, but I was afraid of getting confused with these two different scales. Then a woman would come along and act as an abacus: I'd say one, she'd remember it, then I'd say two. She soon became unnecessary because I didn't make any mistakes. I saw that I was keeping track of the figures accurately. Gradually, I no longer needed to say the numbers out loud. Something fell into place inside me that alerted me automatically every seventy beats. I became a human clock.

Our days lasted between fifteen and eighteen hours, with random variations. From the moment the lights were turned down, which we called the beginning of night, about six hours went by before we were awakened. That was how we estab-lished that we were living according to an artificial clock. We needed to understand why.

Emma put forward the craziest theory.

'We're not on Earth. We are on a planet that rotates every sixteen and a half hours.'

'How would we have got here?'

'How did we get into the bunker?' I asked.

Nobody had the least idea, which amazed me.

I'd put my own lack of memories down to the fact that I'd been so young and to the women's state of shock that Anthea had described to me, but the others knew no more than I did. Apparently, life had been going on as usual, when suddenly, in the middle of a night that had begun like any other, there'd been screams, flames, a stampede, things which I, who'd always lived in the quiet of the bunker, couldn't begin to imagine.

'There were strange drugs that affected the brain and cre-ated false memories,' said Emma.

Anthea wasn't convinced of this. There'd been all sorts of unconfirmed rumours, stories of brainwashing, genetic engineering or robots so sophisticated that they were mistaken for human beings.

'The fact is that none of us seems to have any coherent memories that would enable us to piece together what happened. We don't even know if there was a war,' said Dorothy. 'I can recall only vague images: I see flames, people running in all directions, and I think I'm tied up and frightened. It goes on for a very long time. I'm still frightened, but there aren't even any images any more.'

'Well, I can't even tell you that much,' said Annabel. 'There's my day-to-day life, and then a sort of panic which I've always been terrified of reliving. Then, I'm here, lying on a mattress and everything feels perfectly normal.'

'Wars aren't like that. There are bombs and air-raid sirens.'

'There wasn't a war. Not where we were, at any rate. Of course, those were troubled times, but educated people said that we hadn't lived in peace for a very long time.'

'We were invaded by another country.'

'Or Martians!'

They were as ready as ever to burst out laughing and I began to understand that it wasn't out of stupidity or hopelessness, but as a means of survival.

'So why would they have taken us to another planet? What use could we be to them?'

'Clearly none at all,' chipped in another. 'We're still on Earth. Fifteen or twenty years ago—no, less, you can tell from looking at the child—when we were locked up, there was a purpose, they were keeping us in reserve for something. And then a file got lost, the admin workers made sure no one found out, and they carried on guarding us and keeping us alive, but no one was responsible for us. We're the result of an administrative blunder.'

'But sixteen hours! That doesn't explain sixteen hours!'

'And it's ridiculous that we can't find any pattern in the guards' routine. My memories of before are fuzzy, but I'm sure we worked regular hours. We even had to clock on.'

'Once, only once since I've been counting, the young guard stayed nearly eleven hours at a stretch, pacing up and down around the cage. By the end, he looked drawn and pale, but he didn't complain. I've never seen him looking impatient,' I said.

Our conversations followed these lines, going over and over the same ground. Attempts to recall the early years of imprisonment were fruitless. Apparently, the women had slowly emerged from an inner fog to find themselves accustomed to the strange life they led. There was no suggestion of a rebellion. They'd had husbands, lovers and children. As a result of being too afraid to think about them because it was so painful, they'd forgotten almost everything. But they didn't try to shut me up, because they were horrified at having lost their own history. Anthea gradually became convinced that they'd been drugged.

'Look at us, look at how we live. We have been deprived of everything that made us human, but we organised ourselves, I suppose in order to survive, or because, when you're human, you can't help it. We made up new rules with what we had left, we invented a code. The eldest pours the soup into the bowls, I supervise the sewing, when there is any, Annabel reconciles those who squabble, and we have no idea how all that came about. We must have been living in a dream for a long time and when we woke up, we'd adapted to the situation.'

'What about when Alice wanted to kill herself and Claudia stopped her?'

'That's one memory that stands out amid all the confusion. No one knows when that was.'

I'd been counting for four months. We'd decided no longer to worry about the anarchic routine they imposed on us—my heart would act as our clock. One evening, as the lights were being dimmed, we decided that it was eleven o'clock, and that from that moment, I would count the days as twenty-four hours, as in the past. Sometimes, when we were in the middle of lunch, joylessly eating the boiled vegetables, a woman would ask me the time and I'd reply:

'Two o'clock in the morning.'

That rekindled a spirit of rebellion in their dulled minds. We had our own time, which had nothing in common with that of those who kept us locked up; we'd rediscovered the quality of being human. We were no longer in league with the guards. Inside the bars, my strong, regular heart fuelled by youthful anger had restored to us our own territory; we'd established an area of freedom. New jokes sprang up. When the hatch opened for the second time and we were given a few kilos of pasta, if it was eight o'clock in the morning according to my heart, there was always one woman who'd say:

'Ah! Here's breakfast!'

Or, if it was midnight:

'The show's over, let's have dinner in town.'

And we'd have a fit of giggles. I laughed too, I remember now, because I'd stopped seeing the women as enemies since I'd been giving them what I could: the time. I hadn't forgotten the young guard, and when he was on duty, I continued to watch him, sitting close to the bars, hoping that one day he'd betray himself and give some sign that he'd noticed me, but that did not happen. I still wonder whether it was out of discipline, or whether he really hadn't been struck by the fact that one of the women, always the same one, never took her eyes off him for a moment. I didn't tell myself any more stories.

I'd created the only new thing possible in our static lives. While my gaze was riveted on the young guard, no one disturbed me. Had they done so, it would have drawn attention to me. That left me plenty of time to think. I began to fear that, once again, we would be stultified by habit. It seemed to me that certain discussions no longer aroused much interest, and some of the women began yawning when we tried once again to fathom the rationale behind the time difference. They moaned that we were wearing ourselves out for nothing, that we wouldn't find an explanation, that everything was arbitrary. I told myself that if their enthusiasm waned, I'd start hating them again and feeling alone, whereas I'd been enjoying myself. They'd go back to making jokes that excluded me and I'd be angry again. But Anthea thought I was wrong and that they really had woken up. 'It's even dangerous,' she added. 'I'm afraid that the guards will realise and will drug us again. We'll sink back into apathy, we'll be half dead and we won't even realise it. I can't imagine anything more humiliating.'

Inevitably, with memory comes pain. Sitting facing one another, they found the courage to compare their scant memories. They tried to exhume the past in long conversations which groped their way around the obstacles. They fought against the amnesia which perhaps afforded relief, and against fear. They listened to one another attentively, and when one of them had an idea, she interrupted the woman who was speaking, in a rush to get it out before she forgot it. But they maintained a certain reticence as protection against the tears that would have alerted the guards. I was no longer excluded. I had earned my place among them, even though all I could do was listen.

But this didn't last long, because suddenly, there was a major event.

I must describe the event in precise detail, which I find very difficult, because of the shock and amazement. It happened just as the guards were opening the hatch to give us our food. The pots and pans always stayed inside the cage, we piled them up beside the sinks, but we had to hand back the plates which we slid between the bars after each meal. The food would arrive on huge trolleys and we had to pick it up with our hands and place it in the containers, a task that was both unpleasant and difficult. At the back of the room, on the other side of the bars, a big metal door would slide open a fraction, instantly sparking our curiosity. What would they give us today? What would we be able to do with it? Two of the guards would go over to the door, pulling the trolley, while the third would continue to watch us, his whip at the ready. First of all, we had to take the soup ladle, the forty spoons and the blunt knives for peeling the vegetables. That day, there were carrots and beef cut into coarse chunks, and the women immediately began arguing over whether they would cook all the carrots or keep some to eat raw. There were also potatoes, to our delight, because they were a rare treat. The women said it was odd, because in the past world, potatoes had been very cheap and a food so rich in various things that, according to Anthea, a person could keep healthy eating nothing but potatoes. But we found the quantity of food insufficient, even for the tiny appetites of women who were inactive and had virtually nothing to do, and so the pleasure was short-lived. One of the guards slid a key into the lock of the little hatch. At that precise moment, there was a terrifyingly loud noise.

I'd never heard anything like it, but the women froze, because they'd recognised the sirens. It was an ear-piercingly loud, continuous wail. I was dumbstruck and I think I lost track for the first time since I'd acquired the ability to count time. The women who were seated leapt up, those who were at the bars collecting the food, recoiled. The guard let go of the bunch of keys, leaving them in the lock and turned to face the others. They looked at one another briefly, and then they all rushed towards the main exit, flinging the double doors wide open—something they'd never done before—and ran out.

They ran out. For the first time since we women had been imprisoned, we were alone in the bunker.

For me, the initial shock was soon over. I raced forward, slid my arm between the bars, finished turning the key and removed it together with the whole bunch. I gave the hatch a push and it opened. I stepped back, my hands clenched, because I was holding the most precious thing in the world. My internal clock had started up again and I can say that we stood there for more than a minute, staring at the open door, still unable to grasp what had happened. The shock had taken my breath away and I was panting. I got a grip on myself, grabbed the bars and jumped through the hatch to unlock the door of the cage. There were several keys on the key ring, I had to try two before finding the right one. Since I'd never used a key before, I fumbled, but I managed to open the cage door. The women watched me, rooted to the spot. They looked as though they couldn't grasp what was happening.

'Come on,' I shouted. 'Come on out!'

Then I ran to the other door. I had no idea what I'd find there. It was only a few metres away, which made me wonder whether I'd run into the guards, whether I wasn't rushing head-long into danger, but I told myself that the women would come to the rescue if necessary, and that forty angry women would be more than a match for a few guards, even if they were armed. I went through the open door, and found myself in a wide, deserted corridor. On either side were doors that opened into rooms which I knew nothing about.

The first woman to join me was Anthea, and just behind her, Dorothy, the one who'd questioned me. They both wore the same expression of disbelief. They spoke, but their words were drowned by the continuous wail of the siren, and I couldn't make out what they were saying. I realised that I was talking too, I said that the guards weren't there any more, that they'd left, they'd run away, and things like that. I kept saying the same thing over and over, as if stating an unbelievable truth that had to be repeated again and again to convince myself. We persevered with our futile conversation for a few seconds, then the siren suddenly stopped, as if stifled by its own noise.

'They've gone,' I said.

Dorothy nodded. Anthea echoed:

'They've gone.'

We were so disconcerted that we just stood there, utterly at a loss. Then, one by one, the other women appeared, hesitantly at first, and then, as they reassured each other, they began pushing and shoving, thronging the corridor that was too narrow to contain us all. I withdrew, entered one of the rooms, and looked about me. I saw a big table, a few chairs and some cupboards. Of course, at that point, I didn't know the names of all those things; I saw objects that I didn't recognise as I threaded my way rapidly between them, because I'd glimpsed another door on the far side of the room. It too was open, and led to the staircase.

Today I say staircase as if, at that time, I knew what it was and what I was looking for. As a matter of fact, we weren't even certain that we were underground. The women thought so because there were no windows. I'd never found myself at the foot of a staircase, but I'd heard of them and I immediately realised what this was. I ran up a few stairs then turned round to call, unnecessarily, because Anthea and Dorothy had followed me. They were more cautious than I—later they told me they dreaded the sudden appearance of the guards, and that before following me, they'd shouted to the women that they might have to fight, and the women had replied that they were prepared to be killed if necessary, but they would never return to the cage. I was no longer thinking of them. I ran up the stairs recklessly; I ran with a sort of all-consuming elation, an intoxication akin to the feeling I'd no longer been able to induce by making up stories once I'd emerged from my isolation and begun talking to the others. I was borne by an impulse so powerful that, had a guard appeared at that moment, even if he were twice my size, I'd have knocked him over and trampled him underfoot; I was possessed by a wild joy that was heedless of all else. I climbed without becoming breathless, without getting tired, even though I had never taken more than twenty steps in a straight line. I flew up the steps as in the dreams I had later, dreams I'd heard the women describing, where you rise up and glide like the birds that I was soon to watch being carried by the airstreams, effortlessly drifting, dancing for hours in the twilight, just as I was dancing up the steps, weightless, floating, in an exhilarating ascent towards the undreamed-of unknown, the outside, the world that was not the cage; and I had no thoughts, only a visceral thrill that swept me along, and images, perhaps, that raced through my mind, or simply words that gushed up and rose to receive the imminent images—the sky, the night, the horizon, the sun, the wind, and many more, countless words that had accumulated over the years and which were in a hurry, spurring me on. Oh! That first time I went up the stairs! When I think of it, my eyes fill with tears and I feel that compulsion, that surge of triumph. I think I'd be prepared to relive twelve years of captivity to experience that miraculous ascent, the wonderful certainty that made me so light that I flew up the hundred steps in one go, without stopping for breath, and I was laughing.

All of a sudden, I found myself at the top. I was in what we later called a cabin, three walls and a door, also open, the plain spreading out before me. I bounded forward and looked. It was the world.

It was daylight. The sky was grey, but not the lifeless grey of the bunker walls. Huge masses of subtle hues glided gently in a light breeze. I recognised them as clouds; they were tinged with pearl, lit from behind by the sun. A strange emotion choked me, more restrained and exquisite than the exuberance that had borne me up the stairs. I wished I could linger, but there were too many other things to discover. It was drizzling. Fate would have us emerge on a rainy day. Later, we realised that rain was rare in this season. I stepped forward, raised my face and arms to this extraordinary wetness, which I'd heard about but had been unable to imagine. A few drops fell onto my hands and I licked them, enthralled. My dress was soon soaked through and the breeze, light as it was, plastered it to my thighs, and I found that wonderful.

'But where are we?' asked a voice behind me.

It was a breathless Dorothy, supported by Anthea. They both looked around, and so did I. There was nothing but a gently undulating plain stretching as far as the eye could see, from one end of the horizon to the other.

'We're outside,' I replied, laughing. 'And there isn't a single guard. They've all gone.'

'We're a long way from a town, there's no sign at all of any housing. I'd always thought we must be near some big city,' said Anthea.

Dorothy frowned.

'I've never seen anything like it. This plain is vast, it's unbroken. We are not in my country, you could always see mountains.'

Anthea seemed so puzzled and anxious that I felt sorry for her.

'What does it matter?' I said. 'The main thing is that we're outside, free, and there are no guards.'

The other women began to arrive, out of breath and stumbling, and we moved away from the cabin to make room. Soon, they were all there, looking around in amazement, trying to fathom where they were, repeating, one after the other, that they'd never seen anything like it, almost terrified at being in such a strange place. I couldn't understand why they weren't rejoicing wholeheartedly at the miracle of being outside, released from the cage, at seeing the sky and feeling the wind and the rain. They'd wanted something all their lives, but now they had it, they didn't recognise it. Perhaps, when someone has experienced a day-to-day life that makes sense, they can never become accustomed to strangeness. That is something that I, who have only experienced absurdity, can only suppose.

'I'm frightened,' said Annabel.

They huddled together, a small, terrified group in the middle of an unknown land. After the familiarity of the cage, the forty women clung to one another, disorientated by the vast stillness from which nothing emanated.

'What if they come back?'

I realised they were trying to justify their fear. We scanned our surroundings; all we could see was the stony plain where nothing moved except the scant grass gently swaying in the breeze.

'We mustn't stay here, we must leave, hide,' said Annabel.

'Go where?' muttered Frances. 'There's nothing. Not a building, not a shelter, not a road, just …'

She looked at the small building from which we'd emerged.

'Just this sort of cabin, in the middle of nowhere.'

'We're lost,' said a voice.

There was a murmur of unfinished phrases, one picking up from where the previous speaker had trailed off, their words colliding and tumbling over one another. I suddenly lost my temper.

'Then go back inside! The cage is still down there, if you're so frightened of being outside!'

'Oh, you and your ...' retorted Annabel, exasperated.

She stopped short. I think she was going to say insolence, or rebelliousness, but she quickly realised that I was right, that this panicking would get them nowhere. I tried to control myself too, for I sensed that an argument was brewing, and that would have given them an outlet for their anxiety and set them all against me. Anthea, who'd remained calm, backed me up.

'The child's right. We must think, and organise ourselves. I don't understand where the guards have gone, or why they've disappeared, and I'm frightened too. It's not long since they left the bunker and there's no trace of them.'

'Eleven minutes,' I added, 'since the siren went off—perhaps a little longer, because I lost track of time for a moment. It took us eleven minutes to open the door, get out and climb up the stairs.'

'Eleven minutes? With a helicopter or small aircraft, that's plenty of time for them to vanish from sight, I suppose. But what about us? We can't disappear like that. To get over there, to the horizon, will take us a good two or three hours on foot. If they're planning to come back and catch us, we'll be captured in no time.'

'Not me,' said Annabel. 'I'd rather die, I won't go back. They can drug me as much as they like, I'm sure I could turn the most carefully dosed drug into a lethal poison.'

'Same here,' said Greta. 'I'll stop breathing. It must be a matter of willpower, I'm sure you can stop your heart from beating.'

These words hardened their resolve, they began to chorus: 'Me too', 'Me too'. Rebellion was stirring, it was plain that this time, they would not be caught unawares, as must have happened in the past, that they wouldn't allow themselves to be overtaken by events like terrified creatures who could be led to the slaughterhouse, because they could not conceive of the slaughterhouse. They drew themselves up and gazed at the strange landscape. They planted their feet more firmly on the ground, and there were smiles.

'It's raining,' said Frances.

She held out her hands to collect the raindrops as I had done and raised them to her lips. Then she felt her hair and cheeks.

'I'm soaking wet. I'd forgotten what it's like. It's such a long time …'

'More than twelve years,' said Greta. 'Just look how the child has grown.'

They turned to me, their clock, and stared at me in silence for a long time, then they spread out a little. They bent down and touched the ground. Some of them picked up stones to reveal dry, grey soil, for the rain hadn't soaked through. Annabel moistened her index finger with saliva and held it up to see which way the wind was blowing.

'The clouds are light. It must be the middle of the day, you can see the sun is high. If it is going in the usual direction, the wind is coming from the west.'

'Of course, because it's raining. Westerlies always bring rain.'

'In your country, maybe, but we're not in your country.'

'Oh no! There'd be hills and forests!'

That made them laugh. They needed to relieve the tension.

'It's odd, there aren't any birds. Do the birds shelter when it rains?' asked Greta who'd only ever lived in the city.

'But where would they shelter? There isn't a single tree in sight, only a few shrubs.'

'And stones,' said Dorothy. 'You couldn't grow anything here. I've never seen such poor soil.'

'Anyway, we haven't got anything to grow.'

That short phrase hung in the air for a second, as if minds were grasping it, probing it and then setting it aside for later. But it left an echo:

'We must prepare some food,' said Greta. 'It's time to eat, and I'm hungry. It's funny, because down there, I never felt hungry.'

The food was in the bunker, on the trolley. A shudder rippled through the women at the thought that we'd have to go back down if we wanted to eat.

'How are we going to cook it? I don't see how we can cook!'

'What does it matter? We must eat, even if the meat is raw!'

'I won't go down there. I'd rather die of hunger,' announced Annabel.

Once again, they drew together, shoulder to shoulder, seeking comfort in the contact, I suppose. Someone had to go, and, of course, it was me. Probably because I remembered no other world than that of the prison, I was the least afraid. When they huddled together, I didn't join in, and so I was standing apart from the group, and their eyes turned to me. I understood, and smiled at them:

'Of course,' I said, 'I'll go.'

I lost no time, and made my way immediately towards the cabin. They followed a few metres behind, as if to give me their support in doing what they would have been so afraid to do, and I was glad because I baulked when I reached the staircase. Supposing the guards returned? Would the women be able to fight? For a moment I pictured an appalling massacre, imagining myself coming back up to find a heap of corpses and the sniggering guards waiting for me, brandishing their weapons. I braced myself, because I didn't want to be a coward, and set off down the stairs. Since then, I've been back down hundreds of times—that is one of the few things I haven't counted—and each time it is just as unpleasant, as if I were walking into a trap that could close any minute. When I was alone, I got into the habit of blocking the door of the cabin with a few stones: it was ludicrous, the locks were rusty and the bolts were jammed, and the wind was never strong enough to move the heavy wooden door, but I felt easier.

I rushed down the hundred steps as fast as I could, but taking great care because I'd never descended a staircase before, and I was afraid of falling, then I ran along the corridor to find myself faced with the problem of carrying the huge pots, the carrots and meat, and also the water. I realised that I'd have to make several trips and that it was probably more than I could manage. Half an hour earlier, I'd been so excited that I'd raced up without feeling in the least tired, but now I was short of breath, I felt giddy and my legs were trembling. I reckoned I'd have to make one trip to start with, and so I heaped the meat into a pot. I was halfway up when I met Anthea on her way down.

'I didn't think you'd manage all on your own.'

'You're right, it's too much. Besides, we only thought of the pots and the meat and vegetables, but we also need water, to drink and for cooking, and the plates.'

'And we have to make a fire. Up there, they're gathering stones and twigs, but how will we light it?'

We decided that we'd take up the things I'd already assembled and then we'd explore the rooms.

Later, we thought a great deal about what we'd discovered, but once again, we never came up with a coherent explanation. There were no sleeping quarters for the guards, nor were there any beds, which Anthea found surprising. So they didn't sleep there? Did they leave every evening and come back in the morning? Where did they go?

'They vanished in eleven minutes,' muttered Anthea. 'And we've found no trace of them. I'm not sure an ordinary helicopter can go that fast.'

The drawers contained various tools: hammers, nails, screwdrivers, all of which I had to learn to use, as well as knives and hatchets that would come in very useful. Anthea was thrilled to find four big rucksacks, and she explained what they were used for. Then I showed her a pile of little boxes. They contained matches, which solved the problem of how to light a fire. But, most importantly, we discovered vast stores of food. First it was stacks of cans that made Anthea shout for joy; she read the labels and recited the names of the dishes with an enthusiasm that made me laugh: sauerkraut, baked beans, pâté and vegetables I'd never tasted. Then we opened the door of a cold store full of frozen meat and poultry, as well as sacks of carrots, leeks, celery and turnips. So we'd have no trouble surviving.

'I can't work out how long all this will last, but even with forty of us, it looks to me as if there's enough to keep us going for years.'

She named everything she saw and my head was soon in a whirl from all I'd learned. She would have gone on exploring for hours, but I told her we had to get back to the others, who were waiting for us. We returned with meat, cans, lots of potatoes and matches. The women kindled the twigs stacked up between large stones.

'Dorothy was sure you'd find matches,' said Greta. 'Men always have matches.'

We went back down to fetch some water. This time, two of the stronger women came with us.

The rain had stopped and the clouds dispersed while the food was cooking. The sun came out, high in the sky, which meant, so the women said, that it was the middle of the day.

We ate that first meal sitting in little groups around the fire, whereas, in the cell, each woman used to take her food and sit anywhere. There was plenty of food and, for the first time, there was some left over in the pots, which made the women joke:

'We'll get fat!'

'After dieting so strictly for years, we'll lose the benefit!'

It was only much later that they explained to me why they found that so funny. Strangely, these women who now laughed so readily hadn't joked yet since our escape. I was always solemn, and hadn't changed. I suppose they'd been overwhelmed by the successive shocks.

'What time is it?' Greta asked me.

And I was surprised to hear myself answer that it was ten o'clock at night. It was just over three hours since the siren had gone off, and at that moment, we hadn't been awake for long. So it was true that we hadn't been following the usual pattern of day and night.

'You'd better put your watch right,' laughed Anthea.

'How do I know where to start?'

'We'll watch the sunset this evening. Take that as your starting point and tell us how many hours have gone by at sunset tomorrow. From one sunset to another is a whole day, isn't it?'

'I don't know,' said Dorothy. 'Doesn't it depend on the time of year?'

They launched into a confused argument that went completely over my head. The days got longer in summer, shorter in winter, but from one sunset to another was always twenty-four hours, wasn't it? None of them was completely sure, not even Anthea who was the cleverest. I soon stopped listening to them. Anyway, sooner or later, night would fall: where were we going to spend it?

Of course, there was no question of going back and sleeping in the prison, and the thought of staying close to the cabin wasn't very appealing. I'd watched the sun's progress, and I had the impression that we had a few hours before us until dark. I suggested going down to fetch food and blankets, and then moving away. But in which direction? What if the guards came back? How could we predict where they'd come from when there was no sign of any road? Besides, how had they left? Anthea said there were no beds in the rooms. This provoked a fresh torrent of questions, but Dorothy sensed the impending chaos and reminded the women of what she considered the fundamental question: if we agreed to move away, we had to decide which way to go. So how should we decide? Anthea pointed south: in that direction there was a slight dip in the ground that could conceal us.

The women worried a great deal about the return of the guards, but they never came back. It took a long time for them to shake off their fear, and I couldn't really understand why they weren't reassured sooner. The guards had disappeared in moments, leaving no trace, as if they'd evaporated. They'd appeared from nowhere and now they had gone back there and I was less surprised than the others, who had lived in a world where things used to make sense. But I had known only the absurd, and I think that made me profoundly different from them, as I gradually began to realise. We were free.

In fact, we'd merely moved to a new prison.

Anthea and I made several trips down to fetch everything we needed. The women waited for us outside the cabin and relieved us of our load, then we went straight back down again. The third time, they grabbed us, pleased and excited.

'Come and see! Come and see! Look what we've made!'

A few paces from where we'd sat to eat was a clump of bushes, not very thick, but fairly high. They'd uprooted the bushes in the centre, scratching their hands, and thrown blankets over the sides. We'd brought up two shovels which they'd used to dig a hole. I didn't understand.

'This is the toilet,' they announced triumphantly.

'We're human again,' declared Dorothy. 'We can do our business in private, sheltered from view.'

I was used to the toilet in the prison, and I didn't immediately understand Anthea's delight. There were tears in her eyes. She went over to the makeshift construction, stopped, smiled and asked:

'Is anyone in there?'

They all laughed.

'No, it's free, you can go.'

'This way,' said one of the women, raising a blanket to reveal the entrance.

Anthea went in, lowered the blanket behind her and stood there for a moment. When she reappeared, she told me it was my turn.

The women's complaints about having to defecate in public had taught me a lot, and finally I appreciated the importance of the occasion. I sensed I was being invited to participate in the life of the past, in that world they spoke of together and which I now saw they no longer intended to exclude me from, even though I already knew that I'd never be able to enter it. And so I walked towards the little area staked out by blankets while they watched me with bated breath. I could see they were giving me something very precious, and my lack of enthusiasm bothered me. I drew aside the coarse, stiff fabric, went through and let it fall back into place. At once I had a curious impression of strangeness. My heart thumped, I felt light-headed. I glanced around: I could only see the thorny branches and the folds of the brown-coloured blankets that created a screen between the others and myself. I shivered. But I soon understood: this was the first time that I'd ever found myself alone. No woman could see me, and I couldn't see any of them. I found that very disturbing. I stood there at a loss, contemplating my situation. I discovered physical solitude, something so ordinary for all the others, but which I had never experienced. It immediately appealed to me.

Luckily.

I used the hole, but I felt uneasy because I had to stand with my legs apart, my body half bent over, in an unfamiliar position which I found extremely uncomfortable. I was glad no one could see me in such a pose, whereas I'd never been embarrassed at defecating in front of the other women, happily perched on the toilet seat. Afterwards, I picked up the shovel to cover my faeces as instructed, but I was troubled by the lack of water to wash with and I hoped I hadn't soiled myself. Then I came out. Later, Anthea taught me how to use a handful of leaves.

Greta and Frances overcame their aversion to going back down into the bunker and accompanied us on several trips while the women prepared the bundles. Each of us had knotted the corners of her blanket to make a sort of bag to hold cans of food, meat and various things we thought would come in handy. We set off. The three big pots full of water were each carried by two women and we took turns, changing over often to ensure the water bearers didn't get tired and trip up, spilling the lot. It took us more than an hour to prepare. When we left, the sun seemed to be three-quarters of the way across the sky, and we hoped we'd have time to reach the slight dip before dark.

Anthea and I and the two women who'd helped us were very tired. We'd gone up and down the stairs more than ten times, after years when we hadn't walked more than ten metres in a straight line, and even then, in measured steps, because running wasn't allowed. The others realised, and helped carry some of our load. When Dorothy noticed I was stumbling, she asked if someone would carry my bundle. Afterwards, that never happened to me again, I soon became the strongest, probably because I was the youngest. In any case, I was the one who found it easiest to become acclimatised, probably because I hadn't known anything else and wasn't riddled with regrets.

We were wearing open sandals which impeded our progress because small stones found their way through the holes, hurting our feet and making us limp. Some women tried to go barefoot, but saw that they might graze themselves. It was Laura who had the idea of tearing strips of fabric from her dress and wrapping them round her feet. Soon we had all followed her example.

At the top of the hill, we stopped to look back. Nothing stirred in that vast, arid landscape. We set off again, glancing back frequently, and, as soon as the cabin was out of sight, we wanted to stop, but Greta, who had particularly sharp eyes, said she reckoned there was water down below because she thought she could see the reflections shimmering among the bushes. I'd walked with my nose to the ground, constantly trying not to injure myself despite the makeshift socks. I looked up, but even though I was later to realise I had excellent eyesight, I had no idea what a river running through shrubs might look like. The prospect of water boosted our morale and we decided to go on. Greta hadn't been mistaken, and, half an hour later, we set down our bundles, removed our dresses and ran towards the cool, shallow water.

I loved my first bath so much that I thought I'd never want to get out. I lay on the bed of the stream, my hair floating in the water, for a long time. I'd have fallen asleep if I hadn't begun to feel cold after a while.

We thought we were too tired to feel hungry, but once we had bathed and rested, we did light a fire. The wood burned quickly, soon there were embers and the women made a sort of mesh from wire on which to grill the meat. For the first time, I ate something that hadn't been boiled. It tasted delicious, I felt as though I never wanted to stop eating. In fact, I think I fell asleep with my mouth full!

I awoke in the middle of the night. I was amazed: it was dark! With my eyes wide open, I could barely see my own hands. The sky was a dark mass and rather frightening, as if it might fall in, and it took me ages to realise that once again it was very overcast.

I felt oppressed and tried to reassure myself by remembering what the women had told me about the stars, which are so far away—the constellations and the galaxies. But then another anxiety assailed me, the sense of an infinite void, vertigo, and the fear of falling in this strange darkness, spinning endlessly in nothingness. I curled into a ball as if to protect myself, and became aware that I was lying close to another woman, that I was touching her. That made me start and I instinctively moved away, because of the whip, then I remembered that there were no more guards. All the same, I didn't like the contact with another human body, and I gently moved away. That was the only time I ever experienced the impulse that flung me into Frances's arms that night. Someone had thrown a blanket over me, and I found that strange and touching.

I lay still among the women, my companions in life, who were asleep all around me. A light breeze made the leaves rustle, and I listened to this new sound. I was in a different world, and everything was unfamiliar. Since that morning, I had been learning all the time. I felt a surge of happiness: whatever happened, I had left the bunker, and, like the others, I knew I'd rather die than go back there. Already, I no longer understood how I'd been able to bear living there. I said to myself that if it hadn't killed the women, it was because a person can't die of sorrow.

I saw the sun rise. The sky grew paler as I watched, the clouds dispersed and it grew light—first grey, then golden as the sun climbed higher. I heard birds singing, and I saw some flying high in the sky. Gradually, the women awoke. They looked surprised, as if the night had made them forget that they'd escaped. Then they laughed and called out to one another. We went down to the river to wash and, on exploring further, we came across a place deep enough to swim. Anthea held me in the water, she wanted to teach me breaststroke, but I was terrified. I couldn't follow her instructions and I grazed my knees on the stones. But still, I did manage to float and loved allowing myself to drift along with the gentle current. Then we ate the contents of a few cans of food. The women made a fire and managed to collect lots of hot embers, over which they set the potatoes to boil. We spent most of that first day in this way, eating for pleasure and returning to the river to bathe, time and time again, lazing around in the sun, which wasn't too fierce. But we were still haunted by the fear of the guards, and we decided that two or three of us would keep a constant watch on the cabin from the top of the hill. When it was my turn, I said that I didn't need company. I had a feeling that I'd enjoy being on my own.

That evening, the questions began to rear their heads again: where were we? What were we going to do?

Was this Earth?

They asked me how long it had been from one sunset to the next: by my clock it had been just over twenty-two and a half hours. Clearly, that didn't prove a thing, because we had no idea what my heartbeat actually was. None of the women had ever seen such a wilderness of stones in such a mild climate, but they all admitted that they hadn't travelled much and that in their past lives they hadn't bothered much with geography. Their knowledge was confined to their immediate surroundings and a few local walks near their home towns. Of course, they'd seen films set in countries they'd never visited, but the Earth was so vast! It did seem odd that the vegetation was so sparse—a few clumps of familiar-looking small trees such as holm oak, box-tree and larch, but oh dear! they found it so hard to remember, and an unusual grass. There were no wild flowers, which meant nothing, since it might not have been the right season. They were struck by the absence of insects but were unable to deduce much from that. The terrain rolled towards the horizon in long sweeping undulations but it would be exaggerating to describe it as hilly. But how could we cope with the idea that this wasn't Earth?

'We must look for a town,' they decided.

But what if the towns belonged to the guards? What if we were recaptured? There were countless arguments, which turned out to be in vain, because the fact was we never did find any towns. We were in no hurry to move: the joy of being in the open air, bathing in the river and eating as much as we wanted made us lazy, and we spent several days in idle discussions which the various pleasures soon interrupted.

I no longer felt the furious hostility of before; my anger had subsided. No longer seething with hatred and trying to find fault with my companions, I realised that it was difficult for them to pursue a train of thought for long, or to follow an argument through to its conclusion. Anthea was the only one capable of doing this. Some of the things she said made me realise that their inability to think clearly was the result of having been drugged for a long time. Perhaps I myself could have been a bit cleverer and thought harder than I did when, later, I found myself alone. For instance, it didn't occur to me, after finding the road, to follow it in each direction. That only occurred to me recently, now I'm no longer able to do so. What's more, they weren't very well educated: they were women who, before these mysterious events, had run their homes and raised their children or, if they worked, were shop assistants, waitresses and checkout girls—jobs that were explained to me gradually. Only Anthea had studied: having been a typist for a few years, she went back to college to become a nurse and had qualified just before we were imprisoned. She'd forgotten a lot. The other women lacked foresight and were disorganised. They quickly became routine-bound; they'd never developed skills they hadn't needed. On the whole, that didn't change, and Dorothy, Anthea and I soon took responsibility for our existence.

I'd detested Dorothy because she'd assumed power purely because of her age, but I began to respect her when I saw that she was the first to think about vital matters. Each time the women embarked on a discussion and then lost track, Dorothy would tactfully interrupt them and make a useful suggestion. I saw that her authority came from her wisdom, but I wasn't inclined to wait for orders from her. I preferred to do as she did and think ahead. After a few days, we realised that we had used up half our provisions.

'We must go back and get some more food,' she said, 'and make a list of what is down there. After that, we will decide whether to stay here or leave.'

In her mind, that 'we' still only meant Anthea and her, but I knew it would soon include me.

About fifteen of the women came with Anthea and me. They weren't going to go down into the bunker, but would help carry everything we brought up. It was also suggested they should keep a lookout, which I thought was pointless. I said so to Anthea.

'You may be right,' she replied. 'But I'll feel happier too if there's someone keeping watch at the top. You never know. We don't have a clue as to why they left, or how, so we can't be certain they won't come back.'

That made sense. It is impossible to predict what might happen in a world where you don't know the rules.

So we retraced our steps back to the cabin and, as we drew closer, we fell silent. I'd never been very talkative, but I was used to living amid a steady drone of chatter, and now all that could be heard was the crunching of the stones beneath our feet.

'If we're going to walk, we'll need better shoes,' observed Anthea. 'These sandals won't last two days.'

In our haste to leave, no one had paid attention to the rooms we'd rushed through, but I thought I recalled seeing boots rather like the ones the guards wore.

'The thing is there are forty of us!' exclaimed Greta. 'When you go barefoot, the soles of your feet harden, so perhaps we should …'

But she didn't finish her sentence and nobody started on the usual speculation. We were getting nearer, and a certain foreboding made us silent. We unwittingly slowed our pace.

'Nothing's changed,' said Annabel, as we reached the cabin.

There was a light wind. If we stopped talking and kept still, it whispered the same song in our ears. That day, the clouds were back, the sky was high and white. I saw that my companions were shivering.

'Let's go,' I urged.

We'd been in the open air, and I recoiled in disgust: when we were two-thirds of the way down, the smell hit me. Anthea explained:

'That's our own smell that has lingered. You've already forgotten it. The ventilation system provides air that is breathable, but that's about all.'

Then I heard it: it was the same buzzing noise that I'd heard all my life, and I realised that, since I'd been outside, I'd been vaguely perturbed by its absence.

'And the lights have stayed on,' I noted. 'That's odd. Shouldn't everything have been switched off, stopped?'

'In this world, how can we tell what's normal? Just as well, anyway! We hadn't thought of that.'

The lights never did go out.

Neither of us wanted to enter the big room that housed the cage. But we forced ourselves to, before we did anything else, so as not to spoil the pleasure of exploring. The last traces of apprehension vanished when we saw that everything was exactly as we'd left it. We hoped to take the mattresses, because we'd slept on the ground, levelled with the shovel, joking that we'd lost the only comfort the prison had had to offer.

'They're too heavy,' I protested. 'I don't see how we could carry them if we move on. We can take them up, but we can only use them if we decide to stay put.'

'And that would be ridiculous. We must look for civilisation.'

'What civilisation?'

Anthea looked at me.

'What do you mean?'

I shrugged.

'Just think about it. This planet belongs to them, so what would we find other than the people who held us captive? I have no wish to meet them.'

'You think we're on another planet.'

It wasn't a question, but a statement. I wasn't entirely convinced of what I was saying. I never found out for certain either.

Then we went into the room off to the right, the one that contained a table and a few chairs. Along the wall were six tall, narrow cupboards which Anthea told me were called lockers and were always found in workplaces for people to keep their things in. They were open. In each one, we found two pairs of boots, and I couldn't remember if these were the ones I'd seen. Anthea took them out and placed them on the table. There were also two shirts, two pairs of underpants and two pairs of trousers.

'These could come in very useful. But there aren't enough.'

A drawer contained needles and thread, as well as other objects that I was unable to identify.

'Scissors, buttons and zips—for repairing their uniforms,' said Anthea.

That was all, which she found puzzling.

'No photos, or letters, no personal belongings, but it's true, they didn't live here. They probably kept all that somewhere else. They left in such a hurry, they didn't have time to gather their things.'

She broke off, frowning.

'What's the matter?'

'But if they didn't live here, why the shirts and the boots?'

She shrugged.

We crossed the room where the cans of food were kept to get to the cold store on the other side. Anthea stopped to check the thermometer on the door.

'Minus fifty! This food was meant to last for a very long time. Maybe fresh supplies didn't arrive all that often.'

We quickly took what we needed. I was very cold—a sensation that was completely new to me and which I found painful. Seeing me shiver, Anthea went to fetch a blanket and wrapped me in it.

'You must take care not to fall ill. I don't know what I'd do to make you better, I haven't seen anything that looks like medicines yet. Even though they were always giving us pills! Sit down and rest, I'm going to heat up some water.'

In the other room, we'd seen a small stove and saucepan much smaller than the ones we used. Anthea looked for something to flavour the drink she was making for me and was surprised to find only a few tea leaves in the bottom of a packet. I didn't like this new taste much, but I drank it obediently and it warmed me up.

Then we went back to the first room. Anthea started looking for some coffee, or more packets of tea, but found nothing. I wasn't much help because I couldn't read, and the labels told me nothing. There were a lot of tools: in that department we never lacked for anything, but we had no idea why they were stored there. I have already mentioned the hammer and nails, but there were also saws, planes, all sorts of pliers, picks, shovels and several can-openers. Anthea identified other objects whose names and uses escape me, since I never had occasion to use them.

We took the saws and the shovels. We discovered a huge store of blankets similar to the ones we'd been given, but new. They were probably being kept until they were needed.

'At the rate we got through them, there are enough to last two hundred years!' exclaimed Anthea.

We used them to bundle up the things we were going to take up to the top.

'We won't be able to carry all that, there's too much and we're too weak after all these years doing almost nothing.'

The hundred stairs were daunting enough, but how would we climb them with such a load?

'We could use the trolley,' I suggested, 'if we can get it up the stairs.'

The trolley was heavy and wide. The staircase was straight, so we wouldn't get stuck, but the weight made us dubious.

'Let's try.'

After ten steps, we were out of breath. We had to lift the trolley completely off the grounds so as not to damage the wheels, which would have defeated the object.

'Greta's brave and strong. If she came down and helped, we could manage it.'

We called up, because we were certain the women were waiting for us beside the entrance. Greta willingly joined us. Our progress was slow and we had to stop frequently so as not to exhaust ourselves. When Frances and Annabel saw how tired we were, they overcame their qualms and went down to fetch the bundles we'd prepared. We took enough meat for just two days, since we simply had to come back to get fresh supplies, and we left the mattresses behind because they were too heavy. I carefully shut the door of the cold store behind me and, at the last minute, I picked up a chair for Dorothy.

The return was very slow. We had to clear a path for the trolley and found we were making a little road. Annabel went on ahead to request extra help.

'But this road will tell them where we are!' complained one of the women.

Anthea and Greta shrugged. Gradually, all the women who dared go down concluded that the guards would never come back. There was something so final, such a total absence of any trace of them in the abandoned rooms, that it was impossible to imagine anyone coming and claiming: 'This is mine.'

We quickly organised ourselves into teams: some women went on ahead and removed the stones while others followed, scraping the ground with a shovel. At the slightest obstruction, we halted the trolley to clear the way. Because it was heavily laden, it took several of us to get it moving again. When we arrived, the fires were burning and grilled meat awaited us. Dorothy ate sitting on her chair, and we gathered around her.

'We have to leave,' she said. 'We can't settle here and live from the bunker like parasites. We must remain human beings. I want to know where we are, who imprisoned us and why. I don't want to die sitting on a chair in the middle of I-don't-know-where.'

Curiously, she had just described her fate.

'We have blankets and lots of thread. We'll make rucksacks, and each woman will carry as much as she can. It doesn't matter whether we go north or south, since we don't know in which direction whatever it is we're seeking lies.'

'Nor whether we'll be glad to find it,' muttered Anthea.

'Greta, Anthea and the child will go back down into the bunker to fetch cans. We must assess the weight of what we eat each day and see whether one woman is capable of carrying two months' food. We will walk. We'll build up our stamina, and after a while we'll be able to do twelve to fifteen miles a day, which means six to nine hundred miles altogether. In that time we're bound to find something. Otherwise ...'

She shivered. There was a moment's silence, which was broken by Anthea:

'If we take two months' provisions, we'll only be able to walk for one month. We have to think of the return.'

No one said anything. We didn't want to believe that we'd find nothing. But at night, there were no lights. In the past, there were always signs of human existence—roads, planes— even over deserts. This empty plain and silent sky gave the impression of an uninhabited land.

'We will leave in two days' time. Tomorrow, we'll make the rucksacks.'

That night, the sky cleared. After sunset, when night had fallen, I gazed at the stars for ages. Anthea lay still on her back, her eyes open.

'Are you awake?'

'I'm not sure that this is the sky above Earth. I can't find the Great Bear, which is the only constellation I used to be able to recognise. In the other hemisphere, you could see the Southern Cross, but I don't know what it looked like or where it was.'

The next day, we were very busy. We made several trips down into the bunker to stock up on food; we divided the tools, the shovels and the saucepans into forty piles. Ten women sewed the rucksacks, making them as sturdy as possible. We wanted to take the trolley, but it would slow us down considerably. Thinking back, I can't see why it seemed so obvious that we had to keep it with us. It was as if we all had a foreboding of what lay in store and were determined to deny it. Anthea particularly wanted to keep the wheels. She gave me some complicated explanation about wheels being the origin of all technical processes. Eventually, she found a way of dismantling it. Everyone took a part of it. We would also take the chair with us.

Our progress was fairly slow because of Dorothy and the other two elderly women, Elizabeth and Margaret. We had to stop every hour for them to rest, and when there was an incline, no matter how gentle, they could never make it to the top in one go. I went on ahead, impatient to find out what was on the other side, and was always disappointed, because there was nothing but the plain, a gentle dip and then the next rise. The women watched me return, hoping that I'd have seen houses, a road, a sign, but I shook my head. We made our way across three large undulations, and the sun was going down when we saw another river, smaller than the first, and we decided to stop for the night. We quickly set up camp—the hearth made of stones, a hole in the middle of some shrubs for a latrine, and three blankets for privacy. The meal was relatively silent, disappointment already setting in.

'We should have expected it,' said Anthea. 'They built the prison far from everything, it was probably supposed to remain a secret.'

The women immediately seized on this idea. They didn't want to be sad, and soon found a way of starting a new discussion on the old theme of our captivity. After a while, they even began laughing again. When the sun went down, Rose began to sing.

I was amazed. I'd never heard music before, I was barely aware of its existence. 'Look how beautiful the sky is!' Annabel exclaimed, and everyone turned to watch the sunset. The few cries of delight soon died away, faced with the unexpected splendour of the colours. I didn't recognise them, I'd never seen those shades of pink and mauve, only the grey of the bunker. Long trails of purple tinged with violet … some clouds had a greenish hue, shot through with golden light. The sight took my breath away and I was about to question Anthea when Rose's voice soared up, clear and strong, breaking the silence. I felt a sort of tremor, like a distant echo of the eruption, but it lasted longer and brought tears to my eyes. She sang for a long time, and the other women mouthed the words. The sun disappeared in a sort of long, gentle ovation and dusk settled over the plain.

Later, in my sleep, I felt arms lift me: it was Anthea wrapping me in a blanket. This time, I didn't instinctively recoil at the memory of the guards and the whip, but nor did I go back to sleep. I felt a vague sense of unease. I was distracted by the stars, which fascinated me. I gazed at them for ages, they seemed fixed, and yet they moved, so slowly that I couldn't follow their path. Rose's song still lingered in my ears.

After a while, I went to the toilet. On my way back, I noticed that some of the women were lying in twos, away from the group, entwined under the same blanket. I found that strange. When I had the opportunity to talk to Anthea about it, she shrugged and told me they gave each other what they could. I didn't press the matter, because I could sense she was embarrassed.

We walked for twenty-six days, and every evening there was the sadness and then Rose's singing. She never repeated the same song twice. At first, she sang tunes she'd learned before, then she began to make up songs, developing a talent she didn't know she had. On the twenty-seventh day, when we stopped for lunch, I went on ahead as usual while the women prepared the food, and, for the first time, I spotted something. Halfway down the long slope we'd be heading down after the meal, stood a small, square building that looked so much like the cabin we'd left that at first I thought we must have gone round in a circle. But the lie of the land was different. This cabin wasn't in the middle of the plain and it wasn't facing south like ours, the gaping door was facing me. I raced forward and then realised that I ought to tell the others. So I went back, gesticulating madly, and they abandoned the fires and saucepans to come and join me. I forced myself to wait for them. I too had become a good companion.

They came running up, even Dorothy hurried, despite her shortness of breath. Anthea and I supported her all the way down the hill, and I was glad that this task helped me control my impatience. We stood around the half-open door for a moment, at a loss, terrified: what if there were guards? I stepped forward and pulled the door towards me. The hinges were already rusty and stiff. I pulled harder and they gave way, squeaking. I saw the staircase, the light was on. There was a nasty smell. I went in, with Anthea and Dorothy at my heels, and we started to make our way down. No one spoke, as if a premonition of what we were going to find was beginning to weigh on us.

The smell soon grew stronger and we weren't even halfway down the stairs before it became overpowering. The bravest women were just behind us, and we could hear them exclaiming. Dorothy stopped, tore off the bottom of her dress and made a sort of mask which she held in front of her nose. We all did the same. It hardly lessened the smell but we felt protected from it. We continued our descent, breathing as little as possible, pausing to avoid getting out of breath. One by one, the women had fallen silent, and the only sound was the soft clatter of our feet on the stairs. We reached the bottom. The huge double wooden doors were open, as in our own prison the day the siren went off. I stepped inside and stopped dead, paralysed with horror.

It was the half-light of night-time, but I could see the cage: the floor was strewn with dead women. They seemed to be everywhere, lying across the mattresses, flung on top of each other, groups of them gripping the bars, in heaps, scattered in an appalling chaos. Some were naked, the dresses of others were in tatters, they were in frightful attitudes, tormented, their mouths and eyes open, their fists clenched as if they'd fought and killed one another in the madness from which death had snatched them.

Here, the siren had gone off in the middle of the artificial night, the door was locked and the guards—of course!—hadn't bothered to open it. The women had tried. They'd died of grief, long before hunger had killed them. Without food, furious and desperate, how many days had they spent clawing at the bars with their remaining strength, trying to prise open the lock without keys or tools, their fingers bleeding, trying to achieve the impossible—sick, crazed, lying down exhausted and then getting up again to attack the steel with their bare hands, screaming, crying, dazed, sometimes recovering their wits to contemplate their fate and flee it in fury, and now they stank, distended, putrid and green, infested with maggots that swarmed over their decaying bodies, a grotesque image of the fate that could have been ours, had it not been for an incredible stroke of luck.

Our companions joined us, the first with hasty steps, then drawing slowly to a halt. Anthea, Dorothy and I were gradually pushed back and we found ourselves lined up against the walls of the bunker, as far as possible from the cage, forty live women staring at the forty dead women. We stood there for a long time, speechless with horror, then Dorothy kneeled down and I heard her say softly:

'Holy Mary, mother of God, pray for us poor sinners …'

Later, she told us that she had dredged this up from her childhood, when her grandmother had taught her the Christian prayers without her parents knowing.

The other women also kneeled down and echoed her words, as if, in the face of horror, ancient rituals regained their meaning. The muted drone of jumbled words rose above the terrible jumble of corpses, then Rose's voice could be heard. She sang, and at once her rich, powerful soprano filled the air. I didn't understand the words, but the tone was so slow, sad and profound that horror turned into grief and I felt my heart contract. When she stopped, we were silent, then we left noise-lessly, one at a time, and very slowly made our way back up.

That evening, Anthea explained that Rose had sung the prayer for the dead, in Latin, a language that had been dead for so long that it was only used for ceremonies. I didn't understand, I have still not really understood what a ceremony is, but if anyone ever reads these pages, they'll know.

That day, we stayed put. Returning to the camp, nobody was able to eat and we sat for hours without speaking. It was not until dusk that we ate a little food and began conversing again. So we hadn't been the only prisoners. There was another bunker, exactly the same as ours. These two facts devastated us. We had no idea what had happened to us: at times it seemed as if our discovery would shed some light on things, but at others it made everything seem even more confusing. Looking back now, I can quite simply state that we found ourselves plunged even deeper in the absurd.

I say there were forty of them: we had immediately had the impression that there were as many of them as there were of us, but no one had counted. I did that the next day, to discover that they were only thirty-nine, but there were forty mattresses. One of them had probably died before the day the siren went off and her body been removed. Later, when we discussed it, we still said forty, because they were our equals, our less fortunate doubles. I looked to see whether the bunch of keys had been dropped, we wanted to open the cage to remove the bodies and bury them on the plain, but I found nothing. We tried to force open the bars with the tools we'd brought, but either the bars were very sturdy or none of us knew how to go about it, because we failed. In the end, Anthea and I closed the big double door and that was the only ceremony we were able to give them. We would have liked to make a tomb, and seal it up, or to leave a message saying that, behind these wooden doors lay forty women who had died for some unknown crazy cause, but we had nothing with which to write and the wood was too hard for us to carve.

We made an inventory of the contents of the two rooms as we'd done in the other bunker, and we found the same things, including the boots, which was fortunate because our sandals were in a sorry state. Once again we had fresh meat and we stocked up with canned food.

After three days, we set off again. A sort of inertia had taken hold of my companions. They spoke little, the evenings were silent, except when Rose sang, and they joined in. I believe they didn't want to think, so as not to have to face the inevitable, so as not to despair. They believed they'd find towns, civilisation. I expected never to encounter anything other than cabins, and I think they sensed it. I didn't know the world they described to me, I couldn't imagine it and, when after a long uphill climb I saw only another dip, I wasn't surprised, because I had no clear picture of anything else. But their dejected mood must have affected me, because I lost interest in running on ahead, and it was Greta who spotted the third cabin. We only hastened our steps a little, held back by our apprehension and, as we descended, we didn't hold out much hope that the cage would be open, that the occupants had managed to escape and that we'd meet them one day on the plain. We were greeted by the stench.

We were expecting to find women, but these were men. They too had attempted to escape. They'd tried to loosen one of the sinks and pull away the pipes to make instruments with which to prise open the locks. Everything had resisted their efforts: the pipes were twisted but not broken, the porcelain toilet bowls were lopsided, but they hadn't been able to smash them. The bodies lay scattered everywhere, and were in the same condition as those of the thirty-nine women. The air conditioning was still working. Gradually the smell would fade and the corpses would still be there, mummified or reduced to skeletons, some naked, the others dressed in rags, shirts torn and trousers cut from the same flimsy cloth as our dresses. They'd collapsed all over the place, in all sorts of attitudes, without dignity, tragic witnesses to the incomprehensible. Rose, in tears, refused to come down, and we did not sing the music of the dead. We took everything that might come in useful from the store cupboards and left immediately, walking for as long as we could, so as not to make our camp near a mass grave.

We continued for months, and from then on it was from mass grave to mass grave. We despaired of ever reaching a town. Our expectations had changed: we hoped to find, one day, an open cage. We even decided to leave traces of our visit, to let the others—if there were any—know. In front of the door of each cabin we cleared the ground and drew a big cross, made out of stones. Anthea explained to me that it was the sign of Christianity, the religion of our ancestors, and that a very long time ago, it had been the emblem of the persecuted. No one feared the reappearance of the guards any more, we had no idea what had become of them, but we were certain that they were no longer there. We also made an arrow to show which direction we intended to take.

'But supposing there are others wandering around like us? The cross and the arrow are so obvious that they may well use the same symbols, since they too have only stones to write with! We need a signature,' declared Dorothy, 'otherwise, we might come across our own signs and not recognise them.'

They didn't know what to choose. In the previous world, people used to sign their own names, but forty names written in the dust? Thirty-nine, in fact, because we'd never known what my name was, and the women called me the child. What should we choose? A circle? A triangle? Two parallel lines? In the end, Anthea suggested a cross with a circle above it.

'That will let them know that we're women. What else do we need?'

'There might be other women,' said Greta. 'Let's add something, and, since we don't know anything, not where we are, or why, or where we're going, let's add a question mark.'

This took us an entire day each time. Several of us returned to the bunker where the men were and drew big symbols on the ground. Our bunker and the first bunker of dead women were not marked, but many others were—not all, because I didn't carry on writing the signature on the ground once I was alone. I'd given up believing that any living beings would come.

We walked for two years, advancing in small stages, and then we decided we'd have to stop: Dorothy was growing frail. She was aware of it, but hadn't wanted to say anything. We could see that she was becoming slower and slower. Attempting to get up one morning, she stumbled and at once it was clear that she couldn't stand up. Anthea put her ear to her chest: her heart was beating very feebly. We decided to wait until she was better, but after two days, she grew agitated.

'There's no point waiting,' she said. 'I'm old, I must be over seventy-five, my heart won't get any stronger. We must go on.'

Thanks to the tools that we'd kept with us all this time, we were able to build a kind of stretcher. We felled two trees that were nice and straight, trimmed the trunks and bound the chair to them, using tightly plaited strips of fabric. Dorothy was very weak and felt cold all the time, so we wrapped her in blankets, then we strapped her to the back of the chair and four of us carried her, taking care to walk in step so as not to jolt her. But we only kept it up for a few days because she found even that tiring, and then it became painful for her to stay sitting. We nailed branches across the two wooden poles so that we could carry her lying down. She thanked us profusely, and told us that she felt better, but we could see she was short of breath, and while we moved, she kept her eyes shut most of the time. At first, she slept, and the slightest thing awoke her, then we realised that she no longer reacted when we stopped to change bearers. Anthea said that she'd fallen into a light coma. Some of the women wanted us to stop, but Dorothy woke up and wouldn't hear of it:

'If you stop, I'll say to myself that half an hour later we might have found something, and I'll die angry. I want to keep going until my last breath.'

And that was how Dorothy died, gently rocked by the women while Anthea walked beside her holding her hand. After a while, she could no longer feel her pulse. I saw tears trickling down her cheeks.

'It's over,' she said.

The others caught up with us and we walked on until sunset, thirty-nine women and a corpse, a long, straggling column crossing the plain, a silent procession through the impossible, unwillingly taking possession of the void, alongside the stubborn woman whose wish had been to die without stopping.

We buried her during the night. There was a fine drizzle. Rose's funeral lament hung in the air above the plain.

We stayed by the tomb for several days, as if loath to abandon Dorothy and as if we no longer had any reason to continue. I don't think any one of us still believed in those cities that would be our salvation, or in a bunker where the cage would be open. Almost every evening, Anthea gazed at the sky, wondering where we were. She said that on Earth, we'd have noticed the changing of the seasons, but here, over several months, the days had barely become shorter, and the weather was not noticeably cooler. There'd have been snowstorms or heatwaves, not this unchanging weather, with hardly any rain and this sparse vegetation. Why move on? We wouldn't be any the wiser as to our whereabouts, she said, we'll always be near a bunker and we'll die one by one.

From that time on, I was fully aware that one day I would be the last.

But while we didn't know where to go, we didn't have any better reason for staying, and we set off afresh. So far, we'd walked southwards, and now we changed direction. There were still cabins, bunkers and corpses. When Mary-Jane fell ill, we decided to stop. Until she was better, we said, but we knew it was until she died.

I hadn't had much to do with Mary-Jane, a fairly selfeffacing woman who followed without protest and never made any suggestions. She collected firewood when it was time to build a fire, carried her load without getting out of breath, and was neither among the last nor the first when we walked. In fact, she didn't stand out in any way. I suppose that's what is meant by easy-going. She was one of the women who didn't sleep alone, and she was often seen with Emma, the first woman who thought that this planet wasn't Earth. True there were so few of us that we all knew one another, but certain affinities had created loose groups. I wasn't in the same group as Mary-Jane, but was with Anthea, Greta and Frances, in other words, the group that had formed around Dorothy and which took the decisions. Perhaps that's what they meant by friendship, but in any case, illness brought us all together.

Mary-Jane had stomach pains. One day, she lost a lot of blood, whereas she thought she'd reached the menopause a long time ago, and then the pains started. That night, she slept little, a spasm of pain woke her and its suddenness made her cry out. We all went rushing to her side. She immediately got a grip on herself and we heard her groan, her fists in her mouth, her forehead wet with perspiration. We stood beside her, helpless and desperate. At first, she told us to go back to bed, that there was nothing we could do, but none of us was able to and she eventually accepted our presence.

Emma gently dabbed her forehead with a damp cloth, Anthea placed a hot compress on her stomach which Mary-Jane said was soothing. The attack slowly subsided and she fell asleep, exhausted by the pain. Then we lay down on the ground around her and allowed ourselves to go back to sleep. One morning, on waking up, we saw she was no longer with us.

We'd stopped quite close to a cabin so as to have easy access to supplies. We sat there looking at one another in surprise, seeking her among the others, when it occurred to me to go down into the bunker. There she was. She'd torn her blanket into strips which she'd tied together, then she'd hanged herself from the bars, alongside the forty male corpses. We decided to leave her there. We just cut the rope, laid her out on the floor, carefully wrapped in another blanket, the newest one we had, her hands crossed over her stomach that had hurt her so much, and, for once, Rose agreed to come down and sing in a bunker. Then, we shut the door behind us as we always did. We drew our symbols on the ground and left.

But this time, it was to seek a place to settle down. It was as if these two deaths had convinced us that there was nothing on this planet that was perhaps not Earth. We wanted a river not too far from a bunker that would fulfil our needs: just like the spot we were leaving, but, of course, we didn't want to stay so close to the place where one of us had had to kill herself to end her suffering. Dorothy's death had saddened those who loved her, but she'd been old and it had been a very gentle end. Mary-Jane's death had been a shock, it frightened us. The older women didn't want to talk about it. That was no doubt why we left almost at once.

After a few weeks, we found what we were looking for: the river was wide, in the middle the water came up to our thighs, and there were plenty of trees on the banks. We decided to build houses with large stones and a kind of mortar made of mud. For the roofs, we would use sawn tree trunks. We'd noticed that in some places where the current wasn't so strong, there were water weeds growing. These could be dried and woven together into a rope which we could use to tie together bundles of twigs in a thick layer to make what we called thatch, without being too sure what the word meant. Then we realised that if we mixed those same weeds with the mortar, they made it stronger. We were unpretentious: the sides of the first house were four metres long. It took two months to build and it was very pleasant to shelter inside when it rained. Of course, we couldn't all fit in at once, but the women who stayed outside huddled together to keep warm, as we had always done since our escape, knowing that next time it rained it would be their turn. The second house took less time. We decided to make it rectangular. The trees weren't high and we couldn't support the entire length of the roof with one beam, but we managed to intersect the trunks by supporting them on stone columns, and the whole structure held together very well. Also, we knew that there were never any strong winds.

Perhaps it is still standing.

We brought up chairs and tables from the nearby bunker and, accompanied by four of the strongest women, I went to fetch furniture from the others. We also took mattresses. We often found some along the sides of the cages, which we simply pulled through the bars. We never took mattresses that couldn't be moved without disturbing the dead. When the mattresses had been aired for a while, the smell vanished and they were perfectly usable. Sometimes we made a discovery: a piece of fabric, a store of thread and a bag of sandals which came in handy because, even though we now all had a pair of boots thanks to our pillaging, when we stopped walking we preferred to wear shoes that didn't encase our feet. We'd ditched the trolley because we knew there was one in all the bunkers and that there were lots of bunkers. We found a new one, dismantled it, brought it back and used it to carry our construction materials from one place to another. Altogether we built five houses, and the first became the kitchen. We installed a chimney because we'd managed to make a sort of stove: we hammered empty cans flat, then we bent over the edges with pincers to fit them together and then hammered them down again, thus making a big metal hotplate which we supported on stone walls. We lit the fire underneath and were able to heat several saucepans over a single hearth. I became skilled at sawing and could make planks for building shelves to store our food, as well as benches.

I had very much enjoyed building, and I would gladly have carried on, but the other women didn't want to: after living forty in a cage, they were happy to be nine or ten to a house. They spoke of the facilities in their previous homes, such as running water and baths: those were things of the past that we would have to forget. I had the impression that they found it easier to adapt to our sedentary life than I did. Sometimes, I'd climb a hill and gaze at the plain. I wanted to move on and I became restless. Then I'd think up something to do, an extra table or a bench; the cleverest was a mobile plank system that made it possible to sit on the toilet. I assembled tree trunks sawn in half lengthways to make mobile partitions that could easily be transported, which meant we could do away with the bushes and blankets. It was a long and complicated task which I wanted to accomplish alone. It would have spoilt my fun to have help. When I could think of nothing to build, I'd say that

the saws were blunt, that we needed nails or pliers, and I'd convince one of the women to come with me on an excursion of
several weeks. On our return, I'd come up with a new idea that
would keep me busy for a while, and it always involved making
something or other. But we had so few needs that in the end I
could think of nothing new. The years passed by. Life was quite
monotonous, but one day, a chance conversation with Anthea
aroused my desire to learn.

There were only thirty-eight of us now, living in groups
in the four houses. We'd made what Anthea called bunk beds,
so that the mattresses didn't take up all the floor space. I lived
with Anthea, Greta, Rose, Annabel, Margaret, one of the oldest women, and Denise, Laura and Frances. We were all easy-
going, realistic and seldom argued. The groups that had formed
through natural affinity became more defined when we moved
into the houses, which I understood all too well because I
wouldn't have wanted to be too close to Carol, who was always
excited, or Mary, a sullen woman who was difficult to talk to. I
was still puzzled by the couples. Sometimes there were violent
arguments, with shouting and crying, and I wondered what
could cause so much upset. I had a horror of asking questions,
a hangover from my early years, but Anthea realised that I
didn't understand and she explained to me what women can do
together. I found that strange, for I hated anyone touching me,
which she put down to the memory of the whip.

'In that case, what were men for?' I asked.

She was surprised at my ignorance.

'How can I know if no one tells me? In the bunkers where
there were dead men, some of them were naked and I could
see that they are made differently from us. I suppose that's got
something to do with love. You used to talk about it but we
haven't discussed it for ages, and I'm still none the wiser.'

Then she repeated what I'd heard so many times before:
'What's the use of telling you? There are no more men.'

Anger flared up inside me, but I was no longer a little girl among women: however old I'd been at the start, we'd been out for seven years now and I was certainly over twenty. I was one of the women who thought, who organised our communal life. I'd become skilled, I could saw, nail, sew and weave, and I didn't want to be treated like a child.

'Because I want to know! Sometimes, you can use what you know, but that's not what counts most. I want to know everything there is to know. Not because it's any use, but purely for the pleasure of knowing, and now I demand that you teach me everything you know, even if I'll never be able to use it. And don't forget, I'm the youngest. One day I'll probably be the last and I might need to know things for reasons I can't imagine today.'

Then she told me everything—men, the penis, erections, sperm and children. It took some time, because there were so many things to learn, I forgot details and she had to go back over them. I had a very good memory, but Anthea said that not even the best memory in the world can remember everything at once. She also explained my own body to me. Since I didn't have periods, I didn't know I had a vagina. She was surprised.

'But you must have realised, felt something, even if it was when you were washing?'

Then she surmised that, having started life as I had done, always surrounded by others, I hadn't been able to become intimately acquainted with my own body. Of course, I'd soaped myself carefully, from my anus to my vulva, as the women had told me to do after each visit to the toilet, but those washing movements hadn't taught me that those parts of my body had special qualities. I didn't tell her about the eruption, which I had in fact long forgotten, and it was only much later that I made the connection between that brief thrill and the pleasures of love.

Our conversations were fairly haphazard because often Anthea was so amazed at my ignorance that she lost the thread of her explanations. I imagined my insides. Sometimes she cleared a patch of ground and drew in the dirt. She told me about the stomach, the intestine, and then the heart, the blood vessels and circulation. I was interested in everything and I asked her more than she knew.

'When I was training to be a nurse, I learned lots of things that I've forgotten because I never used them after the exams. Besides, I think that years of being drugged made me forget some of the rest. Dorothy probably died from heart failure. While it was happening, I tried to remember: the weakness of the heart affects the circulatory system, the kidneys and the lungs, it's all part of a perfectly logical system that I used to find so beautiful, but I couldn't recall how it worked.'

'What use would it have been to you?'

'None, you're right, because I didn't have any medicines. I tried, knowing that it was pointless, just because I needed to know. Like you.'

I could feel my intestine, there were rumbles, flatulence and, regularly, stools. My genitals were cloaked in silence. Out of curiosity, sometimes, when I went to the river to wash, I would seek out my vagina: I could barely insert the tip of my finger because of the hymen that sealed it like a door closing off a corridor. I imagined it to be long and narrow, closed at each end, like the corridors in the bunkers: at the entrance, that barrier that only a man can break with his penis, further, the neck of the womb that only the baby about to be born can pass through on its way out of the great room inside. I imagined smooth, soft, dark-red walls, and at the very end, the furthest entrances, the tiny orifices of the oviducts along which, in my body, no egg had ever travelled. Then there was the great fringed foliage of the fallopian tubes which enveloped the ovaries where the most important work should have taken place, the slow and regular maturing of the egg. But my eggs were sterile, perhaps shrivelled, dried up, in this world where they had no purpose. My brain knew that there were no men, and it ordered my pituitary gland not to worry about gonads, it was busy enough with the liver, spleen, pancreas, thyroid gland, bone marrow and all the other tasks that were vital to my survival. There was no point devoting itself to a job that served no purpose. It had not permitted any of my eggs to mature. It had barely allowed my breasts and pubic hair to grow, then it had given up. When I was undernourished in the bunker, my body would have had to compensate for the loss of blood, and it had decided that, with no sperm available, there was no need for the eggs to be released to migrate down towards the uterus. My endometrium was flat. I had never seen a ploughed field because we had no seeds; we had nothing to plant, and my womb would never have to expand to hold a baby, so it wouldn't matter if it shrank or shrivelled up.

While on the subject of couples, Anthea had also explained that there was a way of doing it by oneself, and during my explorations of my body, I wanted to find out what I could get out of it. I allowed my fingers to roam at length over the regions that are supposed to give pleasure: my mucous membranes felt my fingers and my fingers felt my mucous membranes, but that was it. I wasn't surprised, because I'd always suspected I wasn't like the others.

When we were completely settled in what we now called 'the village', I sometimes felt discontented and impatient. I would have liked to carry on looking, but of course, I didn't even know what for, and I tried hard to control my irritability. Anthea had taught me everything she knew: talking with her, I gradually realised that I often made linguistic mistakes which she automatically corrected. She explained what grammar was and I was delighted to discover something new to be learned.

'But none of us is capable of teaching you grammar!' she told me. 'There doesn't even happen to be a primary-school teacher among us.'

'But when you correct me, what do you base that on?'

She thought.

'On habit. And vague memories, rules that I once knew and that I would find it very hard to recall.'

'Couldn't you tell me one, any one?'

I saw her concentrate, as in the past, the first time she had tried to do mental arithmetic. She smiled at me.

'A relative clause is a clause introduced by a relative pronoun and used to qualify a preceding noun or pronoun.'

'Oh! What's a clause? And a noun? And a pronoun?'

I wasn't familiar with any of these terms because, of course, I hadn't learned to speak in a systematic way, but by parroting what I heard. Anthea launched into some rather confused explanations, and called Margaret to the rescue, and then Helen, who'd once tried, with Isabel, to teach me the multiplication tables, and soon there were several of them, arguing heatedly and mustering the little they remembered. They were not averse to the idea of resuming my incomplete education, and they discovered that they too could learn from it. Why didn't they try to speak better? they said. Rose could sing and thus provide us with some precious pleasure, but everybody could speak and find it enjoyable. I was a hardworking pupil. For the others, it was a sort of game which they enjoyed for a while:

we didn't have much in the way of entertainment, and we never said no to anything that was on offer.

The idea of cultivating the few pleasures to which we had access developed. Several of the women took a renewed interest in their appearance and, now we had scissors and combs—Greta had found two in the bunkers—we started looking after our hair. We twisted wire to make hairpins, and Alice, who'd been a hairdresser, made chignons for those who wanted to keep their hair long. But that didn't last, because the combs lost their teeth and we had no way of replacing them.

We also played draughts: that had been Angela's idea. She'd asked me to saw some planks and nail them together. Then she drew boxes using charred sticks and we had to cut small rounds of wood and blacken half of them. They taught me the rules, but I never became a good player because I couldn't see the point of winning a game.

'But it's the satisfaction of being the best, and of using your brain!' said Anthea.

I understood the pleasure of using my brain well enough, but I found it ridiculous to make so much effort just to end up putting the pieces away in an empty box, or arranging them on the board and starting all over again.

We didn't find much else. We would happily have made ourselves clothes, but fabric and thread were still hard to come by. We lived a peaceful existence and, eventually, the lovers' quarrels stopped. The older women were ageing visibly, and they forgot the little passion that had drawn them together. Death made a sudden reappearance: one morning, Bernadette failed to wake up. Like Mary-Jane, she'd been a discreet person, and had remained so right up until her abrupt end, which came completely out of the blue. Then Margaret grew very weak, she lost her memory, could no longer recognise us and was unable to stand. She refused all food except liquids and she became incontinent. Following Anthea's instructions, I built what she called a rack and we made a hole in the mattress, covered with leaves, which we changed regularly, but even so, there was an unpleasant smell in our house, where her life was drawing to a close. Elizabeth, who'd been her lover at the beginning of our wanderings, came and stayed with us, as if her affection had been revived by Margaret's predicament. It lasted for two months, then it suddenly worsened, she became distraught, at night she had bad dreams which made her scream. Then she'd find the strength to get up and run outside, or she'd be seized by terrible rages. That was how she died, shrieking curses. All of a sudden, while she was struggling against the women who were trying to help her, she went rigid staring at Elizabeth, flung out her arm as if to hit her and was wracked by a spasm. She drew herself up to her full height and stated very clearly:

'No, it is out of the question!'

And fell down dead.

We chose a clearing in the middle of the wood as a burial spot, first for Bernadette and then for Margaret. For each of them we made a little monument with a mound of stones and a wooden cross on which we wrote their names. The women carved them as best they could with old knives, after which they burnt in the letters with glowing brands from the fire. The second tomb was dug beside the first, and the women called this place the cemetery. Rose sang. A great sorrow reigned over the village.

Death had begun its work. Who would it single out next time? A vague melancholy set in. I think they were wondering why they were wearing themselves out trying to survive from day to day in this alien land where only the grave awaited them, but they didn't talk about it. They no longer chatted endlessly about nothing, but came and went in silence, slowly, as if weighed down by inevitability. The days went by, and then the months, and the sense of an imminent disaster was dispelled. I realised the day when Elizabeth, who was now the oldest, said to us laughingly:

'It'll be my turn next, and look how active I still am!'

She had just come back from the woods with an armful of heavy branches for the fire and, it was true, she wasn't even out of breath.

Then we started planning ahead again. In the cold store, there was still a large stock of meat, but Helen and Isabel had worked out that with thirty-six of us, it wouldn't last more than five years. I refrained, and I was probably not the only one, from saying that our numbers would decrease. There was no question of replenishing our supplies from another bunker, the nearest was a ten-day hike away and the meat would go off before we got back. The idea of emigrating was floated and I was thrilled at the thought of constructing another village. I had enjoyed building, I started thinking up new arrangements and even became quite excited, offering to add new houses to the village for those who wanted a little more privacy. I had become skilled, but apart from the occasional shelf, I rarely had the opportunity to use my talents. My suggestion was greeted with approval, several of the women who lived as couples said that actually they'd prefer to live on their own. But the most urgent problem was that of our clothing: our dresses were in tatters. We could in fact have gone naked, the climate was so mild, at least during the hottest season, but the women objected. The years of incarceration with no privacy under the watchful eye of the guards had made modesty a luxury which no one wished to forgo. Besides, we had almost run out of soap. We decided to send an expedition towards the west, a direction we hadn't yet explored. Four of us set off, Denise, Frances, Greta and myself, since we were the youngest and strongest. Anthea was probably the same age as the three women who were accompanying me, but she was the nurse, the only one who could understand the women's ailments and perhaps, despite the lack of medicines, find some remedy, so it seemed best for her to stay behind in the village. We were to fetch fabric, sandals, soap and salt, and identify another site in case we did decide to move. Those who stayed behind promised to cut down trees and lay them to dry so that they'd be ready on our return.

It was an enjoyable expedition. We marked the way with big arrows made of stones, so we wouldn't get lost in that monotonous landscape. We went from hilltop to hilltop to get a good view of our surroundings. It wasn't until we reached the ninth bunker that we found fabric, but already in the second, we'd found a packet of coffee. I'd never tasted coffee and I didn't like it very much. I watched my companions shriek with delight and pleasure as they imagined the others' joy when they returned with such a wonderful find, but I was unable to share their excitement. We found as much salt and soap as we needed, but not a single sandal, which upset us, until Denise said we should have thought of it years ago and taken the leather boots to cut sandals from the legs.

'We're not very resourceful, are we!' said Greta ruefully.

'We come from a world where it wasn't necessary, everything was ready-made and we never asked how things were produced,' replied Frances.

They didn't like talking about the past any more than they had done before, and would have said nothing further, but it was a long hike and this was a good opportunity. Because Anthea had taught me a lot of things, I felt bolder about asking questions.

'Tell me what it was like,' I said. 'How did you live?'

Initially, they were reluctant to answer, then they relented. At first, they were talking to me, but it turned out they'd never told one another their life stories, and they were enjoying this opportunity. Frances had been married with two children, Paul and Mary. When the disaster struck, she'd been planning to have a third, and, because her memories were so terribly hazy, she didn't know whether she'd been pregnant and lost the baby or had simply intended to have another child. Her husband was called Lawrence, and she'd met him when she was twenty-three, on the rebound from a love affair which she thought she'd never get over. As she talked, she kept saying:

'But it's all so ordinary, it's the same as everybody else!'

As if she wasn't aware that for me, nothing was ordinary, since nothing had ever happened to me.

'The child's right, nothing's ordinary when it's happening to you,' said Denise. 'I didn't have any children, but I wanted them and I always envied those who did.'

When all their lives had been shattered, she was on her second divorce, because, she said, she always chose the wrong men and was never happy with them. Greta couldn't understand why Denise kept remarrying. She herself had never married, but had lived for years with the same lover and been very happy. That shocked Denise. And they began arguing about whether marriage was a good thing or not. In that wilderness where there were no men to marry, they debated whether it was better to be unfaithful or to leave, and then they burst out laughing. Even I recognised the absurdity of the situation and laughed with them. On reflection, I realise that I laughed a lot more often than I thought. But later, they cried, and I wasn't able to understand them any more. Then they felt sorry for me, because I'd never experience love, and it was the same as when they talked about chocolate or the joys of a long, hot bath; I believed them without really being able to imagine what they were talking about.

Greta had had a son by this man she'd never married, but apart from naming them, none of them would ever talk about their children. On that subject, my questions were unable to break through their defences. Later, Anthea tried to explain their reticence to me.

'You can't understand, and since I didn't have any children myself, I probably don't fully understand either, but just think about what might have happened to their children! Growing up alone, like you, among strangers who weren't in a position to take proper care of them? Or killed? Or dumped in groups of forty in bunkers, living like animals, dying for want of attention? They don't want to think about their children. They're probably all dead, and better off that way. If Frances was pregnant, she must have had a miscarriage. You've never seen a child, you don't know what it means—their vulnerability, their trust, the love you feel for them, the anxiety, being ready to lay down your life to save them, and it's unbearable to imagine a child's pain.'

It's true I know nothing of all that and have no memories of my own childhood. Perhaps that's why I'm so different from the others. I must be lacking in certain experiences that make a person fully human.

I don't remember their accounts very well, probably because there were too many things that I hadn't experienced and couldn't picture. They'd say: 'We went dancing.' What was dancing? They explained, they formed couples, facing each other. Denise placed her left hand on Frances's waist and held her right hand up in the air, then they spun around. Yes, but what about the music? The sound of an accordion or a violin?

They spelled out waltzes, one, two, three, one, two, three. Having counted my own heartbeats for so long, I could understand a repetitive rhythm, but I could never imagine the sound of the band, nor the laughter of those boys who made them lovesick, nor the rustle of chiffon or silk dresses swirling around them and making them look so beautiful. They spoke of creeping home at dawn, angry parents who scolded them, kisses, jilted lovers, men they were in love with but who didn't love them, and it was all a muddle in my head. Gradually, I stopped asking them to tell me about their world, and I gave up trying to imagine it. I knew very well that I came from it. I'd had a father and a mother who probably went dancing and got married or left each other, and were torn apart by the disaster like Frances and Lawrence. Perhaps one of the dead women I'd seen in the bunkers was my mother, and my father was lying mummified near the bars of one of the prisons; all the links between them and me have been severed. There's no continuity and the world I have come from is utterly foreign to me. I haven't heard its music, I haven't seen its painting, I haven't read its books, except for the handful I found in the refuge and of which I understood little. I know only the stony plain, wandering, and the gradual loss of hope. I am the sterile offspring of a race about which I know nothing, not even whether it has become extinct. Perhaps, somewhere, humanity is flourishing under the stars, unaware that a daughter of its blood is ending her days in silence. There is nothing we can do about it.

Such thoughts ought to make me weep. But tears never come to my eyes except when I think about Anthea, a woman I actually knew. I cannot mourn for what I have not known.

Every evening we'd collect a huge pile of dead wood and make a fire. We grilled sausages coated with mustard, of which we'd found a few jars, and we ate them with flour cakes baked over the embers. We were relaxed and tired, and I think that for a while, my companions' nostalgia was allayed as they experienced the vast silence of the plain, the continual rustle of the grass. We were in no hurry to sleep, we listened to the breeze which always whistled the same soft note. Apart from Rose's powerful soprano, it was the only music I'd ever heard.

Sometimes, as I returned to the group around the fire, I'd feel a rush of emotion; I was moved by the flickering of the flames in the night, the silhouettes of the women resting, the interplay of words or Denise's reedy voice carrying the laments of another era across the plain, and I understood what Anthea called beauty, which apparently had been so abundant in their world.

After four months, we set out for home. We'd gone round in a huge circle, so it only took us a month to return to the village. We were slightly apprehensive, but there had been no deaths. The timber promised for the new buildings was ready and we set to work. I enjoyed it immensely. We'd found two excellent sites to move to if we decided to leave our present settlement, but that seemed unlikely because I could see that the women were happy in their new houses and wouldn't agree to leave until the cold store was practically empty. All the same, when the houses were finished, I went on a quick expedition with Anthea to the nearest place: the river was nice and wide, rich in aquatic plants, with a clayey bed which she said might be useful for making bricks. There was a small wood, vital for timber. 'I don't know whether you've noticed that there aren't many trees left,' she said. 'They don't grow very fast and we may run out of wood before we run out of meat.'

Shortly after our return, Angela announced that she was unwell. She had giddy spells, memory lapses and a feeling of exhaustion that rest could not cure. She didn't think she was older than sixty or sixty-five, but she came from a family where people didn't live to a very old age, she told us, and, should the situation arise, she didn't want us to allow her to suffer or deteriorate as Margaret had done.

'What do you want us to do?' protested Anthea. 'I understand what you're asking and, if I had syringes and medicines, I'd promise anything you like. But here?'

'There are the knives,' replied Angela. 'You know just where to strike to pierce the heart.'

It proved unnecessary. She soon fell into a coma and died within three days, but the idea took root in Anthea's mind. She thought of Mary-Jane who'd gone off to hang herself in the bunker.

'You see, it keeps haunting me, gnawing at me. She fled all alone in the middle of the night, and perhaps she cried out in pain while making her rope. I feel I abandoned her. Angela was right: I know where the heart is and how to plunge in a knife to stop it. I think that if anyone else suffers the same pain as Mary-Jane, it will be my duty to do what is necessary, but I'm afraid of being too cowardly.'

'You can teach me,' I said. 'I could do it. I'm not like the rest of you.'

The thirteenth year after our escape, we decided to move because we'd almost run out of meat. Several more women had died and now there were only thirty-two of us left, but these deaths had always happened either quite quickly or calmly and I hadn't yet had to carry out my promise. With the few trees still left and the trolley wheels, we built makeshift carts on which we loaded the tables and chairs. We went to a site that was a three-week trek from the first village, and we built ten houses. The first one was as big as possible, and the others were smaller, to accommodate just a few women. It was a huge task but one which, naturally, gave us enormous pleasure. We had become good carpenters and our roofs were sound structures. We even managed to make excellent bricks with mud from the riverbed, and our walls may not have been completely straight, but they held up. We tried to make gardens around the front doors by gathering a few of the rare wild flowers, but they always died, no matter how carefully we watered them.

Greta, Anthea, Frances and I shared a house. Most of the women were living as couples, except for Denise, Annabel and Laura who set up as a threesome. But we only built one kitchen and we ate our meals together, at tables arranged in a big square. Once the village was built, which took a good year, we began to dread idleness. Some of the women had really taken to woodwork and I went on several expeditions to find other types of tree or thicker trunks. Sometimes, I found a hollow branch which I'd bring back for Rose. She wanted to carve a flute, but was never satisfied with the result. None of us had learned the simple things, such as pottery, or the art of recognising herbs, and Anthea said that even a land as arid as this ought to provide more resources for creativity than the things we'd thought of so far. For example, if properly treated, the aquatic plants we'd used for making thatched roofs could perhaps be used for knitting and weaving. Frances remembered that flax had to be retted, but what was retting? Another woman suggested letting the wood soak for a long time and then bending it. But our efforts were fruitless, and after a few disappointments we gave up.

Gradually, the futility of all our attempts dampened our spirits. Our bed and board were guaranteed, a few metres of fabric satisfied our modesty, and a few kilos of soft soap met our hygiene requirements. We were going to die one by one without having understood anything of what had happened to us and, as the years went by, our questions petered out. The lights in the bunkers were still on, and I simply couldn't resign myself to never understanding anything. Where did the electricity come from? There had to be a power station operating somewhere, Anthea had told me. Was it entirely automated? Were there still some people who operated it without knowing why? Would it stop one day and the meat rot in the cold stores? No one dreamed of seeing rescuers appear, and the few remaining questions were always about our failure. I didn't dare admit that I wanted to carry on walking and exploring, because I knew they'd think I was crazy.

Our mood was not one of despair, which Anthea explained to me was a violent feeling that led to great emotional outbursts, but rather one of equanimity. There were no longer extensive conversations on every subject, nor the nervous jollity of before. During the year when we were building the new village, the women had become animated again, but then they lapsed into the old sluggishness, never hurrying to complete any task, since there were so few that they preferred to draw them out. That made them seem like old women. They had no reason to look up, so they walked with a stoop. The last passions had fizzled out, their hair was going grey and they seemed to have lost the desire to live. We had survived the prison, the plain and the loss of all hope, but the women had discovered that survival is no more than putting off the moment of death. They continued to eat, drink and sleep, while in the shadows, surrender, silent capitulation and death lurked. They became thin, the furrows on their dejected faces grew deeper, they easily became breathless, their hips were painful and their legs swollen. Elizabeth suffered from haemorrhages, Greta stomach pains and Anna became paralysed down one side of her body.

She could no longer speak, one eye was closed and the other begged. We all knew what she was asking, but Anthea, weeping, was unable to grant it.

'You told me that you'd be able to do it,' Anthea murmured, not daring to meet my eye.

'I'll do it,' I told her.

I didn't really understand. If that was what Anna wanted and we could offer her no other relief, why was it so difficult for them to act? I think I understand them now that I have cried, but I can't be sure, because even though I've spent most of my life with them, I am well aware that I was always different. I'm probably missing a chunk of their past.

She had explained everything to me in detail. You had to count the ribs down from the collarbone, then find the edge of the sternum and go back three fingers. She showed me on her own breast the exact spot where I would have to plunge the knife in hard, with a single swift stroke.

'Then, when it's my turn, you'll know what to do.'

They all went out of the house where Anna lay and I was left alone with her. I sat beside her. She looked at me and I saw, on what remained of her face, that she was trying to smile at me. I drew back the blanket from her emaciated chest, and had no difficulty in counting the protruding ribs, nor in locating the edge of the sternum. I placed my finger on the spot and I could feel the beating of her heart, which seemed vigorous. It was certain that if we did not intervene, she could remain the victim of this appalling condition for a long time. She raised the arm she was still able to move and stroked my cheek while I placed on her skin the point of the knife that I had spent ages sharpening. I was swift and accurate, her arm fell back and her heart was beating no more.

I received that caress several times—the only one I was able to tolerate—the silent gratitude of a woman receiving death at my hands. None wanted to endure pain and I think they were in a hurry to die. I don't know how many I killed—I who count everything, that was one thing I didn't count. Each time, even when they were contorted with the most violent pain, I saw their tormented faces relax as I was about to strike, and it didn't make me cry because I sensed their haste and their relief. It was only at the moment of death that they admitted their despair and rushed headlong towards the great, dark doors that I opened for them, leaving the sterile plain where their lives had gone awry without a backward glance, eager to embrace another world which perhaps didn't exist, but they preferred nothingness to the futile succession of empty days. And I know that at that moment, they loved me. My hand never trembled. We became strange accomplices during their last moments, when I was the chosen companion, the one who would unravel their incomprehensible fate, closer than their forgotten lovers, dead in the bunkers or under another sky, closer than their weeping lovers waiting at the door for me to come out, the knife wrapped in a thick rag that would conceal any drops of blood, and nod my head confirming that it was all over, that the sick woman's suffering was at an end, and that, at least for one of us, the agony was over. Then we could hum the song of death. Afterwards, we'd gaze at one another for a moment in silence, then the women would go inside and shroud the dead woman in a blanket, the newest and best one we had. At nightfall, we'd carry her to the cemetery and lower her gently into her grave. One after the other, they were buried under that sky and neither they nor I knew if it was the one under which we'd been born.

It wasn't necessary for me to stop Anthea's heart. Each death had contributed a little to killing her. There had been so much hope when we'd escaped from the prison, and then this slow dissipation, the gradual abandonment of all expecta-tions, a defeat that had killed everything without a battle. She wondered when it had dawned on us that we were as much prisoners out in the open as we had been behind bars. Was it after finding the second bunker when we'd been terrified at the sight of the thirty-nine dead women, heaped up or collapsed on top of one another? Or the first time we'd descended a staircase with no further hope of finding the cage open? Or when Mary-Jane had hanged herself? When did we know for certain that we had no future, that we would continue to live as parasites on those who'd locked us up, stealing below ground to take our food from the departed enemy? And how was it that we hadn't died from sheer nausea? She mulled over these questions endlessly, and I listened in silence. The impossibility of finding any answers fuelled the grief that was killing her. When there were only six of us left, and Greta died, Anthea no longer had the strength to stand and had to be carried to the cemetery. We used a litter like the one on which Dorothy had died, and Anthea lay on her back gazing up at the sky as we walked, still wondering if it was that of planet Earth. There was a moon. The women always said that it looked like the moon they'd known, but they weren't sure they could trust their own memories. Anthea's sight had grown poor, she screwed up her eyes with a futile persistence. When we arrived, Greta was already lying in her grave and Laura was keeping vigil. Rose had passed away, but the women had learned the song and their voices resonated for a long time over the plain, because they repeated it several times. I had never sung. We hadn't sung in the bunker, and afterwards it was too late, I had a lump in my throat. Nor could I shout, I could only produce a raucous croak that didn't travel far. I do not know whether I am still able to speak. Of course, all I have to do is try, but I don't seem to want to. And what does it matter if I've become mute in a world where there is no one to talk to?

We stood at the graveside for a long time, in silence. From time to time, one of the women would repeat the terrible words:

'From the depths, I call on you, O Lord.' Perhaps that isn't exactly the right translation, none of us really knew that dead language which they chanted over a land that was almost dead, but they'd told me what they understood. Their voices soared up, they gazed at the dark sky as if they somehow expected a reply, but nothing ever crossed that vault except the silent movement of the stars. Then, one after the other, they fell silent, the chorus died out like an untended fire, and silence descended, barely ruffled by the lightest of winds that permanently blows. All that was left for us to do was to throw earth over the emaciated body that was barely discernible under the blanket and then make our way slowly back to the village of empty houses.

The women placed the litter next to the bed and left us alone. I settled Anthea in her bed—she'd grown so thin that I could lift her easily. I covered her well because she'd become very sensitive to the cold, and we bade each other goodnight. But I could hear her crying, and I was unable to sleep. I went over and sat on the edge of her bed. She asked me to hold her hand. She knew how much I hated touching anyone and I understood that if she was asking me to overcome my revulsion, it was because she desperately needed this pitiful contact.

'You know that you are going to end up alone,' she said.

I often thought about it.

'I looked after you as best I could when you were little, and later I taught you everything I knew. But soon I won't be there for you any more. I feel as though I'm deserting you.'

'You have no choice,' I replied.

'How will you survive?'

'I'll move on. I'll carry on looking. If it had been up to me, I'd never have stopped, but I could see that the others couldn't go on any more.'

'Will you be able to cope? Won't you go mad?'

'I have no idea what you mean by madness. You know I'm not like the rest of you. I haven't experienced the things you miss so badly, or if I ever did, I don't remember anything, and that hasn't done me any harm. To me it feels as if I've always been alone, even among all of you, because I'm so different. I've never really understood you, I didn't know what you were talking about.'

'It's true,' she agreed. 'You are the only one of us who belongs to this country.'

'No, this country belongs to me. I will be its sole owner and everything here will be mine.'

After that, she lay silent for a long time. I suppose she was thinking about the old days, when she'd led a life that made sense and that she had lost, because sometimes tears ran down her cheeks, and I wiped them gently away. Otherwise, we remained still and I could feel her irregular heartbeat, even in her hand. I'd learned to recognise that kind of rhythm, which gets weaker and weaker. You think it's stopped, but it starts up again, but there's no hope; life isn't tenacious enough to win. I wasn't sure that Anthea would see the dawn. At one point in the night, she asked if I could bear to cradle her in my arms.

'I'm so cold.'

I offered to go and fetch another blanket. She nodded and smiled feebly.

'I need to be held.'

That cost me an effort which I'm certain I managed to hide. I lay down beside her and she rested her head on my shoulder, and I clasped her to me.

'I have loved you so much,' she told me.

She drifted off into a light sleep, and I think she dreamed, because she sometimes made little movements and muttered indistinctly. Day was beginning to break when she grew completely calm. She was breathing very softly. I wasn't afraid of falling asleep, and I concentrated my attention on her ebbing life. I didn't know exactly when she stopped breathing, we were both so tranquil and silent. Death is sometimes so discreet that it steals in noiselessly, stays for only a moment and carries off its prey, and I didn't notice the change. When I was certain it was all over, I lay there for a long time, holding her to me, as she had wanted.

It was all I could do.

Frances, Denise, Laura and I were the only ones left. A few months later, Frances had a fall in the house and broke her legs. Anthea had explained to me about these fractures in elderly women, and there was no chance she would recover. Frances was in such pain that she didn't even want us to lift her or make her more comfortable. She asked me to stab her immediately, she didn't want to suffer a moment longer than was necessary. I left her alone with Denise and Laura while I ensured that the knife was as sharp as possible. On my return, the two able-bodied women rose to leave the house, and something strange happened: they both stopped as they passed me and hugged me, as if they were thanking me for what I was about to do. I knelt beside Frances, who gripped my shoulders and pulled me towards her, to place a kiss on each of my cheeks.

'You are kind,' she said.

That touched me. I smiled at her and she was smiling as the knife went in.

On our return from the cemetery, Denise asked me to do the same for her, but I don't know why it was impossible for me to do it to a woman who was still in good health, even if I knew how much grief she was suffering. She had to wait three years, when she became semi-paralysed, like Anna, except her face wasn't affected and she was able to talk.

'Now, will you?'

'Now, it's different. I must do it.'

And so I remained alone with Laura. Apart from me, she had been the youngest of the women and her death didn't seem imminent. Although she'd accompanied me on several expeditions, I didn't have a spontaneous liking for her. She was rather grumpy and was constantly complaining. When we were alone, her personality changed. She never protested at my decisions and, to be honest, it would have required a lot of imagination to protest against what I exaggeratedly call decisions. If I said it was time to go and fetch some meat from the nearest bunker, wash our clothes or light a fire, it was always because we were getting low on meat and our dresses were dirty. She appeared to let herself be completely guided by me, and I realised that she'd lost all interest in her life.

One morning, as I was returning to the village laden with cans of food, I was struck by her absent air. It was the season when it rains the least and I'd put the bench outside the door. I found her sitting there, staring into space. For years, her eyesight had been poor, and now, she was gazing into the distance without even screwing up her eyes, although she said this helped her distinguish things. Her hands were resting on her thighs, but with her palms upturned, as if she'd forgotten to turn them over, which made her look strange, neglected, a woman plonked there whom nobody had taken the trouble to tidy up, like a garment dropped in a hurry lying crumpled on the floor. Her thighs were slightly apart. Before, in the prison, Laura had been thin, like all the others, then she'd grown fat, complaining all the time that she couldn't control her appetite. But since the death of her lover, Alice, she'd lost interest in food and had shed a lot of weight. Now she'd resumed the attitude of a corpulent woman whose knees didn't touch when her legs were together, because of the size of her thighs, as if her body no longer recognised itself in the present. Her dress had ridden up slightly, revealing her withered, fragile flesh. I was the one who'd made that dress, meticulously assembling scraps of fabric that were still usable from the least worn tunics, and she'd watched me work, as if she couldn't really understand why I busied myself so. Then she'd put on the dress and recovered her wits for a moment to thank me. We'd always been very particular about manners, even back in the bunker—probably to differentiate ourselves from the guards and their whips.

I went up to her, talking so as not to give her a fright. I told her that I'd brought back some soup, that we could eat soon, and some soap because our last packet was nearly finished.

'But I was right, I looked everywhere but there's no more thread, I shan't be able to mend your dress.'

In the past, we'd used her hair to sew with, but now our hair had stopped growing and was short and sparse.

As I spoke to her, I was thinking that I'd have to go on an expedition because we were going to run out of soap too, but I held back from saying so. I was only talking for the sake of it, frightened by her expression that was so vacant, so absent, that she looked as if she was asleep with her eyes open. She started violently, turned her head towards me and, as she'd told me before, must have seen only a vague shape.

'Oh, it's you, child,' she said as if she'd forgotten that there were only the two of us left. 'You're a good girl. I'm not much help to you.'

I said a few comforting words and went inside to light the fire. She followed me slowly and stood beside me. She watched me, seemingly unable to think of a way to help.

'Do you think I'll live much longer?' she asked.

Her tone was calm and normal. She was asking an ordinary question and would happily listen to the answer and then think of something else. Surely such a lack of interest in her own concerns could only be a sign of impending death?

The women had only ever called me 'child', and even now that I've been alone for such a long time, and because I have no other name, I still have a vague feeling that I am the youngest, even though there is no one left with whom to compare my age. I thought back to the days when I'd been furious and full of contempt, when I'd had the impression that they were laughing at me, that I knew nothing and they knew everything, and I found it heart-rending to see that Laura was now consulting me as if I were an oracle. She just stood there, not knowing what to do with her body.

'Do you feel ill?'

I had been so slow to reply that she must have forgotten her question. She looked taken aback, struggled to think, and nodded.

'I'm tired. But everyone's tired, aren't they?'

Everyone: the two of us.

'Yes, everyone,' I replied calmly.

If she didn't remember that everyone was dead, why remind her?

The fire had got going. I put on the logs, covered it and picked up a saucepan. I chose two cans containing tomato soup. Anthea had taught me to read the labels and I was delighted to discover that they were the kind that contained little meatballs. Laura stood beside me, as if she couldn't think what else to do. Her legs seemed unsteady. It wasn't very obvious, and I wasn't certain. I told myself at first it was her disorientated air that made me think that, but since she stopped living shortly afterwards, it's likely that she was finding it hard to stay on her feet. I led her gently to a chair at the big table, sat her down and placed a bowl and glass in front of her.

'We'll be eating in a few minutes.'

'If you like,' she replied.

I looked at her carefully. Her face was utterly devoid of expression and it was probably my own anxiety that made me think she looked lost. Her eyes had a glazed look and her arms dangled by her sides. I wanted to place them in her lap, but that reminded me of the gesture I'd made so often, crossing the arms of a dead woman on her chest, and then closing her eyes, so I held back. But at the same time I was certain she was dying.

Like that, on her feet, without being ill? It wasn't her body that was giving up, but her spirit, which had grown increasingly weary of animating those muscles, of making that heart beat, of going through all the motions of living, the spirit that nothing had nourished for such a long time, that had watched its sisters die and that had for its only companion a woman who disliked her and whom she disliked. How tragic! I said to myself. How tragic! She had, in the past, lived out twenty or twenty-five years of her legitimate destiny, and then crazy events had taken place and she'd entered a world of absurdity, surrounded by strange women who were as confused as she was. Despite all that, she had tried to love. I thought of Alice, a lively, impatient woman, who used to say to me: 'Go away and play!' when I disturbed her and then apologised. They'd lived together in a little house. They argued noisily and made up again with great promises: you had to do something to pass the time. I sat down in front of Laura, I sincerely wanted to say some helpful words that would sustain her, but, to be honest, in this sterile land, in the silence and the solitude, ignorant and sterile myself, what could I give her? Why should she want to live? We were doing nothing, we were going nowhere, we were nobody.

'You see,' I said to her, 'I want to go off exploring. I don't want to end my days here, eating canned food only for it to come out again later.'

She looked up. You could see she was trying very hard to understand what I was talking about. Then, to help her, I said:

'I'm going off exploring.'

'But there's nothing,' she said, surprised. 'Only the bunkers.' Thinking was a great effort for her.

'There aren't even any seasons.'

'We don't know. We gave up too soon. We only searched for two years, didn't we?'

'That was because of the old women. We had to keep stopping so they could die in peace. And sometimes they took such a long time. They kept feeling better and we thought they'd recover.'

'I want to leave. I'm not old.'

'Wait,' she said. 'Wait. I shan't be long.'

She understood me. We both knew that she couldn't cope on her own, that she wouldn't have the strength to go and get food from the bunkers or gather enough wood for her fire, and that I couldn't abandon her.

The soup was hot. We ate in silence, then I went to wash up in the river. When I returned, she was sitting on the bench again, waiting for me. She'd sit then until she felt sleepy and then would go and lie down on her mattress to sleep. While asleep, she'd be waiting to wake up.

I didn't want her to die, but how could I have wanted her to live? Several times during the afternoon, I felt a tremor of impatience. I was overjoyed at the idea that I was going to be free. To calm my excitement, I began working out what I'd need. I'd take one of the big bags and pack enough provisions for two weeks, two blankets—because I'd grown used to sleeping on a mattress and I was afraid I'd find the ground too hard. Later, when I'd adjusted, one blanket would be enough and my load would be lighter. I'd need lots of matches, a small shovel and boots. I must remember to take some soap. My dress was in complete tatters, but I'd be bound to find some fabric and thread, because I'd regularly come across bunkers with fresh supplies. I'd have to make sure I found the right size boots if I wanted to walk a long way. In the past, I'd had the unpleasant experience of blisters, and for years, I'd been living in sandals. We'd never found any socks and the skin of my feet had become soft, but I knew it would soon harden.

I bustled about, devoting myself happily to the too few domestic tasks, and my mind busied itself planning the route. I kept going over the list of things I needed to take, enumerating, repeating, summarising, to the point where I began to feel very irritable. Soon I'd have done everything it was possible to do: the floor was swept, the mattresses turned, the blankets shaken, there was nothing left to wash or put away. I went out and sat on a chair facing Laura. She was staring at the sky, at the point where the sun would set later, and her gaze was more vacant, more absent than ever. Her breathing was even. Her hands were once again resting on her thighs palms upturned, and I could see a tiny artery pulsing on the outside of her wrist. It was regular, clear and strong. That's why I don't think she died of a physical illness, but that she abandoned her unflagging body which would have carried on for years, except for her eyes. She heard me coming, muttered a few words, so softly that I didn't understand, but I didn't feel like asking her to repeat them. What could she have to say to me? What did we have of the slightest interest to tell each other? That it was a fine day, that it was unlikely to rain that night, that the sun was going down? She was no more interested in telling me than I was in hearing it, and most likely she'd only attempted to speak to me out of politeness, to show that she was glad of my company, which was probably not entirely true. What could I give her, other than food and drink, which would only prolong an existence she no longer desired?

'Yes, of course,' I said.

That satisfied her. We were in agreement, without being too sure over what. Or perhaps over the fact that we had nothing in common. And so we sat in silence.

I didn't watch the sky. I was fascinated by Laura. She seemed to be disappearing inside herself, withdrawing further and further. At first, there was still some expression on her face, the ghost of the smile she'd given to welcome me, a hint of weariness, a faint grimace when an insect settled on her hand. She didn't budge, I brushed the creature away but she seemed oblivious. The setting sun illuminated her face. There was no shadow, nothing to see except for skin, taut over tissue that was still living, a live model, with peaks and troughs, different from those of a plain or a hill, that the eyes could explore but without learning anything other than their configuration. I could have touched her, for sure, run my hands over her cheeks, but would she have felt it? There was a moment when everything was as if suspended. I could see clearly that the little artery in her wrist was still beating, but I was certain that Laura was dead. Her breathing was soft and regular, with an automatic rhythm that was unable to stop, but she was no longer thinking. In the past, Anthea had explained what an electroencephalogram was: Laura's would have been flat. Sitting on the bench, gazing towards the setting sun, she lost her mind in the cerebral convolutions, the mysterious nooks and crannies of the memory, she had gone backwards, seeking a world that made sense, losing her way among the labyrinths, slowly deteriorating, dimming, noiselessly being obliterated and then fading away so gradually that it was impossible to pinpoint the transition between the flickering little flame and the shadows. As the sun touched the horizon, her wrist stood out clearly in the evening light and I saw that there was no more movement under her white skin. I let out a deep sigh. My last tie had been cut.

I sat looking at her for a long time, then I lay her on the bench and crossed her hands on her chest, carefully placing her palms downwards. I didn't have to close her almost blind eyes, which had shut of their own accord. There was no reason to delay. I picked up the shovel and went to dig behind the big house, where the others were already buried. It was a very clear night, as always when the sky was cloudless, even though there was no moon. I didn't need to dig a very deep hole since there were no animals to come and unearth the bodies, and I wouldn't bother to leave a mound or sign indicating that the remains of a human being lay there. I would remember, and there was no one else to tell. The grave was ready in an hour. I had to carry Laura there. I'd thought about it while I was digging. I was alone and even though she'd lost weight, I doubted whether I would be able to carry her. I found the thought of putting her on the trolley repulsive: it was too short and her legs would swing grotesquely, whereas I wanted to transport her in a dignified manner. I was in a real quandary, and it was only when I went back to her that the idea came to me, when I caught sight of the big table that I'd made such a long time ago. I would balance it on the trolley, then I'd place Laura on it, carefully shrouded in the best blanket. It was very difficult, and I suspected that years of a sedentary existence had sapped my physical strength. It took all my determination. Night had long since fallen when I was ready to accompany Laura to her grave. I went to pick a few wild flowers to scatter around her face, as the women had done. She was pale, and at peace, looking no more dead than when her heart was still beating and she had lost interest in staying alive.

I began to push the trolley. I had to stop frequently, to remove stones and sweep the ground, it was a slow funeral procession, this burial of a woman by the last remaining woman. I stopped, leaned over and straightened up again. I remembered the descriptions of pilgrimages I'd listened to, of those people who went around churches on their knees, begging forgiveness for their sins. I'd never really understood what that was all about, but I sensed I was participating in a very ancient ritual belonging to that planet from which I'd come but which was so foreign to me.

'There,' I said to Laura's corpse when we arrived. 'It's almost over.'

I picked her up as gently as I could and it bothered me less than touching a living person. She seemed terribly heavy and I found it very difficult to lay her down without jolting her, but I managed it. I didn't want to cover her with earth, crush the peaceful face and the white hair which I'd carefully smoothed. I slid the big table to the ground and pulled off the legs, then placed the top on the grave. I levelled the earth all around and stepped back: it was a fine, clean rectangular tomb. The rain, rare as it was, would doubtless bleach the wood, but it would stay put and Laura could quietly turn to dust.

I went to bed. After all that effort, I thought I'd sleep like a log, but I was too excited by the idea of my departure. At around three o'clock in the morning, unable to wait a moment longer, I got up, rekindled the fire to heat some water, and began packing. When there had been thirty or forty of us, we always had to take into account the old women, who walked slowly and couldn't carry much, but I was strong and I decided to take three weeks' worth of supplies, which was more than enough to last me until I came to another bunker. Over the years, we'd found six metal gourds, which I filled with water, because rivers were few and far between. It was sometimes several days' walk from one to the next. Anthea had told me that meat gave you strength and I had seen, when burying Laura, that I need to build up my stamina again. The cans didn't contain enough, so I decided to go and get some from the cold store and boil it for a long time so that it would keep.

We'd settled five kilometres from a men's prison and had, as usual, closed the main door—a humble ceremony which we never failed to accomplish. When I'd taken out my supplies of meat, I wanted to have a last look at my dead companions of the last ten years. With time, the stench had gone, because the air conditioning was still working. As we went from bunker to bunker, I'd grown used to the sight of now mummified bodies piled haphazardly. However, one caught my eye. He was sitting apart from the others, a long way from the locked door. Had he wanted to cut himself off from the frenzied group that had attacked the lock until their very last breath, or had he died last, after dealing the final blow to those who could stand it no longer but were unable to stop living, as I had so often done? He had folded a mattress behind him and two on either side, so he was sitting up very straight, his body firmly supported. He seemed to me to have died proud, holding his head up high, his big eyes staring at the dark passage, with an air of self-respect and defiance. I walked around the cage and went close to him: despite the little left of his face, I had the impression he must have been handsome, the dark beard and withered skin didn't mask the beauty of his features. His fists were clenched, resting side by side on his knees, perhaps this was how warriors of the past died, weapon in hand, looking their fate in the eyes. His torso was half clothed in a torn tunic, I could see the powerful bones of a shoulder that must have been strong. I felt a surge of grief, I, who had never known men, as I stood in front of this man who had wanted to overcome fear and despair to enter eternity upright and furious. I sighed and left.

I climbed back up slowly, because I felt a strange nostalgia calling me back. I would never go down into this bunker again.

Oh! I would see a hundred others, there were so many of them, but in this one where I had so often come for supplies, I'd never taken the trouble to look at the withered corpses, and now one of them affected me. I hadn't noticed him among his companions, and when I finally did see him, I was about to leave. In another life, I might have met him. He wasn't very old, he could have been a friend of my father's, or my father himself, since I had definitely had a father. Or even a lover. But all I knew of him was his intention to die with dignity, sitting erect, apart from the others, away from the pushing and shoving, the fears and cries in which the others were enmeshed. He was a loner, like me, a proud man, and I was leaving, knowing nothing of him other than his final plan. But that at least he had achieved. He'd wanted to face his destiny to the last, and someone knew it. As long as I lived, my memory of him would live too, there would be a witness to his pride and solitude. I stopped, hesitated for a moment, then went back down to gaze at him for a long time. There was nothing new to be discovered on his parchment face. I felt a profound sadness. I told myself that that was perhaps how, in the time of the humans, people said goodbye to the body of a cherished lover, by trying to engrave them in their memory. I knew nothing about him, but I knew nothing about myself, except that, one day, I too would die and that, like him, I would prop myself up and remain upright, looking straight ahead until the last, and, when death triumphed over my gaze, I would be like a proud monument raised with hatred in the face of silence.

Reluctantly, I bade him goodbye. Back at the village, I boiled my meat. Because I had to keep stoking the fire, I couldn't go to bed. Dawn was about to break, and I still didn't feel sleepy. In the prison, sleeping had been compulsory, and I later discovered that it was necessary for one's well-being and also that it was advisable to keep to the same pattern as every-body else. But I was alone. Nobody was dependent on me any more, and my habits would not disturb anyone. I had complete trust in my body, which would demand sleep when it needed it, so there was no reason for me to go to bed if I didn't feel like it. I could leave. I put on my shoes, slung on my rucksack and went out. I didn't even need to put out the fire, lock up the house, or tidy away the few things I was leaving behind. All I had to do was decide which way to go.

I walked towards the rising sun because the sky ahead was magnificent. There wasn't a cloud to be seen, and I loved watch-ing the day unfold. I set out at a relaxed, unhurried pace, which I'd be able to keep up for a long time. I took my bearings from the landscape and began the trek which I intended to continue as long as I lived, even if I didn't know what I expected from it. I walked up the long, gentle slope towards the east, and turned round when I reached the top. I gazed at the ten houses in the village which I'd so enjoyed building. Behind the biggest one was the cemetery where I'd buried Anthea. Only now, I tell myself that what I'd felt for her, the trust that slowly built up, the constant preference for her company and the joy each time I was reunited with her after an expedition were probably what the women called love. Now, I had nobody left to love.

From the start, I counted my steps. My heartbeats had been my unit of time, my steps would be my unit of length. I'd been told that an average step was seventy centimetres, and that there were a hundred centimetres in a metre. When the women spoke of lengths or distances, it was always in metres or kilometres, so I tended to use the same concepts. I soon realised that was completely ridiculous—those terms had meaning for them, but not for me, and I no longer needed to use a shared language. An hour's walk—that meant something to me. I didn't need to go to the trouble of converting my steps to kilometres. I would evaluate distances in hours' walking. I always relied on my confidence in my inner clock and, during that first day, I decided to count the number of steps I took in one hour and to choose a unit that would be my equivalent of the kilometre. So I had to walk at a very regular pace. The ground wasn't very hilly, alternating between gentle descents and moderate inclines which probably made little difference to my speed. My first stop was after five hours. I'd counted thirty-seven thousand, seven hundred and forty-two steps. I embarked on a division operation that I now found less difficult since Anthea had shown me how to do it by writing the numbers in the dirt, but all the same it required an enormous effort of concentration. That came out at seven thousand, one hundred and fifty steps an hour. I decided to check by counting hour by hour, and then by fractions of ten minutes, and ended up, by the evening, with the discovery that I walked regularly at a pace of a hundred and nineteen to a hundred and twenty-two steps a minute.

At the same time, I tried to evaluate in advance how far it was to a particular point, so as to give myself a sense of distance. The monotonous landscape didn't help, and I had to be content with a bush, a small rock or some other little landmark. Sometimes I was unsure whether the bush I was walking past was the one I'd selected ten or fifteen minutes earlier or not. But I measured the distance I covered and I could feel myself acquiring a sense of distance, as I had once felt myself acquiring a sense of time.

That first day, in spite of my sleepless night, I walked for ten hours, at my even pace which could take me a long way, and decided to stop as soon as I felt that tiredness was slowing me down. I wondered what would make me stop, whether it would be hunger, sleep or boredom—in other words, what prompts decisions when you are utterly alone. I was satisfied by this first answer: I wanted to create an internal distance meter, and so it was my plan and my determination to carry it out under the right conditions that governed my decisions. I sat down at the spot where I had felt my pace slacken. I could have gathered a few twigs and branches from the nearest shrubs and lit a fire, but as soon as I'd put my rucksack down on the ground, I realised I was exhausted and decided to eat my boiled meat without heating it up. True, it wasn't a very appetising meal, but it was pleasantly seasoned with the feeling of having complete freedom at last. I was able to gauge just how much I'd resented having to give in to the other women's wish to settle down, and I smiled to myself as I thought of the immense journey awaiting me. I flattened the ground, stretched out on a blanket folded in half, rolled myself up in the other one and fell asleep at once. After six hours, I woke up, starving, ate again and fell asleep until sunrise. Before setting off again, I scattered some earth over the hole where I'd relieved myself, then I noticed that I was stiff all over. My ankles, thighs and back ached. I had certainly never walked for such a long time at a stretch. I didn't know what to do about it. Should I wait and rest, or carry on in the hope that the exercise would relax my muscles? The prospect of spending a day sitting in the middle of that boring plain seemed ridiculous and my impatience got the better of me. But, since I couldn't rely on the regularity of my speed, I wouldn't try to perfect my distance meter that day.

In the afternoon, the landscape changed slightly. The long undulations became more marked, there were slopes that measured a good ten thousand steps. It would be exaggerating to describe them as hills, but I was very excited at the idea that this variation could be the beginning of a hilly area. I wanted to speed up my pace, which seemed even more unreasonable given that, although my aches and pains had grown no worse, they hadn't gone away either, and I suspected that I shouldn't be reckless and risk being unable to walk at all. Besides, tiredness got the better of me earlier than the previous day and I didn't want to overstretch myself. I was certain that you don't build endurance by pushing yourself beyond your limits. I stopped just before six o'clock in the evening and made a fire. I ate a lot, as much and for as long as I could. Before going to sleep, I rubbed my feet with fat because they were hot. One of the cans contained what the women called bean and bacon casserole, with a layer of lard on top which I removed before heating the rest in my saucepan. I'd noticed that when I got this fat on my hands, it softened my skin, and that's what gave me the idea of using it on my feet, and I also put some on my face. I didn't fall asleep as quickly as I had done the night before, and I watched the sun set and the first stars come out in the pale, smooth sky.

In the middle of the third day, I saw that there was a cabin on the next slope. I hadn't expected to come across one so soon. I stopped, sat down in the sparse, dry grass to contemplate my goal from afar. I knew only too well what I'd find there—the eternal procession of despair. At the top, the rusty locks, the lights permanently on, and, down below, the locked prison, the cage and its population of corpses. I'd go down and look at everything very closely. That was the only tribute I was able to pay the victims. And then I'd close the main door. I don't know if I still hoped to find an open cage one day, or come across the traces of another group of women or men who'd escaped and settled outside, as we had done—only the traces because, as the last survivor from my bunker, I didn't imagine that others would have lived any longer than my companions. I thought about it because I was in the habit of considering every angle of a question, and I'd never had any form of entertainment other than thinking.

The sun was going down when I set off again. The rest had done me good and my aches were gone. I'd reckoned the bunker was half an hour away, and was pleased to find that I wasn't mistaken: I reached it in twenty-eight minutes. I put my rucksack down inside the cabin and made my way down the stairs without hurrying. There was almost no smell, but I still tried to breathe cautiously. The women had compared the stench with that of a sewer, of insalubrious marshes or a cesspool—none of which I had known. For me, it was simply the faint smell of corpses. Down below, in the narrow corridor, the doors were open to reveal the usual layout: the guards' room, the cupboard at the back, the big double doors of the prison. I saw a chair had been knocked over and a saucepan overturned, spilling its contents which had dried leaving a brown stain. This slight disorder was rare and aroused my curiosity, but first of all, I had to go and see the cage. We had always felt this was an obligation, even when we'd become certain that we would never find the door open. We had to pay our respects to the dead, to those contorted bodies that lived there, piled haphazardly, perpetual inhabitants of horror and silence.

They were women. I stared at them for a long time, then I walked around the cage taking in everything: there was nothing new. The knives, forks and plates were still in the cage, revealing that here, when the alarm had sounded, they'd been eating. A whip was lying on the floor of the area where the guards had paced up and down. One of them must have been rather more jumpy than was customary and had dropped his weapon. Perhaps he was the one who'd knocked over the chair as he fled. The whip was lying against the wall, out of reach of the prisoners who'd tried to grab it to the very end. One was slumped against the bars, her arm still outstretched, overcome by death during her final attempt.

The guards' room contained only the usual items: chairs, a table, lockers. Absolutely nothing had been left behind. Anthea had often told me she found that odd, but I didn't really understand. I possessed nothing, so I couldn't imagine the objects she told me about: books, letters, cigarettes, playing cards, razors. I travelled with two blankets, a small shovel, a can-opener, matches and food, and so I didn't find it surprising that the guards only had their clothes and their weapons. I righted the chair, sat down and felt sad. I hadn't wanted to look at the dead women, but I forced myself. Apart from the one with her arm outstretched, I hadn't really seen them. I told myself that I'd been hypocritical and, since I had no one to lie to, I discovered that you can lie to yourself, which felt very strange. Was I missing companionship more than I thought and making myself into another, a witness, if only to deceive her? I pondered this thought for a long time, but I couldn't see how to develop it further. I was as much a prisoner outside this empty land as I had been in the cage during my early years. I gave up this futile avenue and resumed my usual train of thought, which was always to plan, assess and organise, and went to investigate the food store. That was the only thing that varied from one bunker to the next, as if deliveries had comprised large quantities of the same thing and the choice of how these were used was left up to the guards. In the cold store, I found large hunks of beef which I'd have to defrost before I could cut them up. There was no pork or mutton left. In the cupboard were several tins of powdered milk, which thrilled me. It was at least three years since I'd last had any, and I knew that it was a very nourishing food that would help build up my strength. I was interested in some other tins of powder. At that time, my reading was very poor and I found it hard to decipher the labels. When I managed to do so, I was puzzled by the word 'orange'. Of course,

I'd heard the women say it and I gradually recalled that it was with nostalgia for one of the good things of the past. I diluted a little of the powder in water and tasted it with curiosity. I found it rather bitter and needed sweetening, but I rarely had any sugar. But Anthea had told me about vitamins and I took the tins thinking that they'd improve my diet.

I made several trips down into the bunker to bring up the meat, the powders, a mattress and a chair. I cooked a copious meal and had the brainwave of sprinkling my mixture of meat and vegetables with milk powder. After that, I slept for a long time. When I awoke, I realised that there was nothing more for me to do there. I felt vaguely disappointed, as if I had hoped for more from that bunker, as if I'd forgotten that they were all the same. The next one would also have the door locked, but I'd be unlikely to find more milk there. Perhaps there'd be some other novelty? The women had talked of chocolate, bread and cheese. I was looking for something else. I told myself that, while waiting to find out what it was—because I was modest to the point of not thinking 'before finding it'—I would enjoy the lovely red meat that I could grill over my fire of twigs, and also the milk, of which I drank a whole gourdful.

At around eight o'clock in the morning, I felt wonderfully good. I went down into the bunker to fetch a few cans to replace the ones I'd used in the past few days and to see if I could find some thread, which I'd forgotten to do the day before. By the time I was ready to leave, my rucksack weighed a lot more than when I'd arrived, but it didn't feel too heavy. I was already a lot stronger and I wanted to take the mattress with me, because I'd slept much better than on the ground, but I told myself I ought to be careful, and that there'd be plenty of time to think about that in a few days, at the next bunker, when I'd completely adjusted to my new life. Perhaps I would no longer need it.

I didn't leave the usual signs on the ground as I no longer believed there might be any other survivors. But I discarded the mattress in front of the cabin so that if I came that way again, I'd recognise my own traces.

I think I have given an accurate account of this first bunker. I think so, but I can't be certain. I'm sure that was the one where I found milk, but afterwards, which one was it where I found tea? The fifth? The tenth? They were all the same, with their forty mummified corpses piled up or scattered across the floor. Only once did I find thirty-eight, and only once did I find all the women lying calmly, as if they'd understood that death was inevitable and had decided to wait in silence. Another time, the keys had fallen within two metres of the bars and I thought how dreadful it must have been to see them without being able to reach them. Sometimes, a tap was running in the cage, making a little trickling sound that startled me at first, but I'd already lost all hope that the door would be open. Each time, there was the food store and the permanent light. I travelled eastwards, from one bunker to another, carrying my provisions, and in the end, I never did take a mattress. My shoes wore out, which didn't bother me—eventually I was bound to find some boots to fit me. Then came the season when the sky is always cloudy, with the fine drizzle that I knew well, and I was glad to find a waterproof sheet in one of the guard rooms. It was folded on the table, beside a pile of new blankets which hadn't been put away. That set me thinking again about how rare it was to find unusual objects in the bunkers, as if it had been decreed that they all had to be absolutely identical. I was about to plunge into my habitual speculation about the guards and the meaning of our imprisonment. At first, I felt like shrugging and turning my thoughts to other things. But why? How else would I occupy my mind? After our escape, Dorothy used to say: 'Let's organise our life, let's not waste our thoughts.' The fact was, I could use my thoughts as I pleased, the idea of wasting them was absurd. My survival was guaranteed, I would never exhaust all the food available, and the rare bad weather had never made me ill. I could allow my mind to wander as it pleased, it didn't matter if the paths it took were dead ends—all I had to do was put a stop to them. It was certain that the purpose of our deportation and captivity would never be revealed to me through the abandoned objects, and the whip lying on the ground taught me nothing useful. I found the same thing in all the bunkers, even in the guards' quarters.

Even in the guards' quarters: I don't think I'd ever formulated that so clearly. Those words kept haunting me and were beginning to annoy me, when at last an idea began to form: we had understood that the guards didn't want to give us any clues as to the reasons for our captivity and our being kept alive, but we'd always assumed that they knew. What if they were as much in the dark as we were? What if they were forced to do a job that they weren't permitted to understand? What if by putting the same things in all the bunkers, those in charge wanted to keep all information from them as well as from us? I was electrified by this theory, I could feel my footsteps dancing and I began to laugh. I was perfectly aware that I had only added another question to all the others, but it was a new one, and, in the absurd world in which I lived, and still live, that was happiness.

I would be the sole proprietor of this land, I'd said to Anthea shortly before she died. But I knew that the stones and the cold stores would constitute a paltry treasure. I'd set out with the intention of discovering things—possibly the power plant the women had always talked about, the place from which the orders that governed our lives were issued—anything that was new. To think that the guards knew nothing was a new idea, and to me nothing seemed more precious. I would have liked to celebrate. Since I lived as I pleased, walking, eating and sleeping when I felt like it, I couldn't invent anything special, but that evening, I lit the fire and grilled my meat with a light heart. I promised myself sweet dreams that night. I don't know if I had them. Every night, I had plenty of company, and, on waking, I always had the vague recollection that I'd been laughing and playing with women and men, but I never managed to remember anything more specific. That always surprises me because when I am awake, I forget nothing.

Having realised that, in fact, the guards were also victims, I was prepared for the strange encounter that awaited me. I'd been walking for a year, always in the direction of the rising sun. The landscape had changed a little, the long undulations had become hills, and I never climbed them without hope. The rivers were deeper and it was possible to swim in them, which gave me immense pleasure, and I saw new types of tree in the denser woods. I carefully examined the bushes, because I remembered that the women had spoken of wild berries—strawberries, blackberries and raspberries—which all tasted delicious, but I never saw anything that resembled their descriptions. Once, I came across what I thought must be mushrooms, but I didn't pick them because they'd said that they might be poisonous. It was on leaving one of these woods that I was struck by the lie of the land.

A long valley stretched out ahead, covered with the usual scrawny vegetation and loose stones, but I could immediately make out a strip that looked different: the grass was even sparser, there were virtually no stones. It formed a straight trail to the next hilltop. The women had spoken of roads: could this be one? I went down towards it, deciding of course to follow it, even if it wasn't heading eastwards, since I'd only chosen this direction to avoid going round in circles. I walked for a day and a half before reaching the summit of a long, low hill. As soon as I looked down, I saw the bus.

I say bus, but of course, initially, I didn't know what I was looking at. First of all, it was half an hour away and all I could make out was a rectangular shape in the middle of the plain; and then, naturally, I'd never seen a bus. All I had to go on was what the women had told me, and none of them had given me precise descriptions of things that they took for granted. I only knew that it was a vehicle that could carry a lot of people.

My heart was racing as I ran down so fast that I was at the bottom in ten minutes. I stumbled a couple of times, because I couldn't take my eyes off my goal: a huge rusty structure which was ten paces long and twice my height, standing on wheels that were mostly broken, with windows all around. As soon as I was halfway down, I could see the figures sitting in the bus, and I nearly stopped dead in my tracks, but I quickly got a grip on myself. I ran up to it, dropped my rucksack and stood rooted to the spot, trying to take in what I saw. I recognised a door with a handle, and I tried to turn it, but it came off in my hand. The panes were broken, I tugged at the frame, the door opened and immediately dropped off its hinges. I hauled myself up what remained of the steps and entered the bus.

Over the years, the corpses in the bunkers had mummified; these had become skeletons, dressed in the all-too-familiar uniform, equipped with their weapons and strange masks which hid their facial bones. They were sitting naturally, as if death had struck very suddenly and they'd slipped, without being in the least aware of their last heartbeat, into that final immobility where, for years, nothing had disturbed them. The driver was in his seat, his hands still gripping the wheel. On entering the bus, I'd raised a light cloud of dust which settled around me as I stood there dumbstruck. I mechanically did what I'd been doing for years and which had become the very structure of my mind: I began to count. I enumerated twenty-two passengers on the twenty-four seats, sitting in pairs on either side of a central gangway. So there were twenty-three bodies. Each one had a kit bag, either on his knees, or on the floor between his feet. Incredulously I made a careful check: there was no sign of panic, nothing suggested that they'd been forewarned of any danger. The bus had stopped in the middle of the plain and they had all died on the spot.

I stood looking around me for a long time, allowing my wild curiosity to satisfy itself at its own pace. I already knew that it would remain frustrated—I could count myself lucky if this bizarre world that I inhabited was kind enough to add a few more questions to my list of unanswered ones. It was five o'clock and the sun had begun its descent before I was stirred into action.

My interest was primarily in the kit bags: I had explored more than a hundred bunkers but I'd never seen these bags made of coarse, stiff cloth, with straps and metal buckles. I picked one up. Impatience got the better of me while I was taking it outside, I was tense and my heart was pounding. I tried to calm down, telling myself that I wouldn't find anything extraordinary, but I didn't believe that, and my fingers trembled as I undid the knots.

On top was a carefully folded garment, of a kind I'd never seen. It had long sleeves, a stiff collar and a belt, and it wasn't cut from a fabric I'd ever seen before, but from a thick, fairly supple material with creases, pockets, flat seams—the word came back to me at once—and padded parts. I was used to light cotton that fluttered in the slightest breeze and I thought this must be uncomfortable to wear. It was probably a jacket, a garment the women had mentioned but which the men had never worn in the bunker.

Underneath, there were several items. I began with a smaller packet, made of thick paper. Obviously, I didn't know it was paper, because I'd never seen any, but I shan't go into the difficulties I had in identifying and naming all these things because that would be too tedious and I wouldn't enjoy it. I'd have to repeat myself over and over again. I undid the packet carefully, it was fragile and threatened to fall apart. It only contained a brownish dust, odourless and tasteless, probably some sort of food that had dried up. Then, from a small soft leather pouch, I took out a strange instrument that I had to examine closely to find a very thin blade sandwiched between two metal plates, all mounted on a handle that was very easy to hold. You couldn't use it for cutting unless you removed the blade: it took me a long time to guess that it was a razor. The third item was a glass bottle, which I put to one side as I was much more intrigued by two pieces of carefully folded, big white rectangles of thick, supple fabric. I thought they must be those towels made of terry cloth that the women missed so badly and which I'd learned to manage without. But I could use them to make myself something to replace my tattered dress. There were also two pairs of knickers. I remembered later that for men, the word underpants was used.

And underneath, a book.

Anthea had taught me the alphabet and the rudiments of reading by drawing the letters in the sand. At the time, it bored her, because she couldn't see what I would do with such knowledge, but I had insisted: there was too little to learn for me not to grasp at everything I could. I had words in my head for things I'd never seen, let alone touched, as I was now doing.

I recognised the book at once and I was so overwhelmed that I felt almost giddy. I think that if I'd been standing, I'd have collapsed. I had in my hands the most precious of treasures, a spring from which to drink the knowledge of that world to which I would never have access. As always when I was overcome by emotion, I began to count. The title, written large, had twenty-three letters divided into four words, all beginning with capitals. I looked, without trying to decipher—excitement, impatience and tiredness were a bad mixture which made me tense and dulled my mind. I no longer knew which way to turn, whether to satisfy my curiosity and search the bags or to find out what the book was about, and I had to make an enormous effort to control myself. As the sun was already very low and soon I wouldn't be able to see enough, I decided to save the book for later, but my excitement made me clumsy and I dropped the bottle that had been in my lap. It was sheer luck that it didn't break, as it had landed on the jacket and I was able to catch it before it rolled onto the stones. That calmed me down and I resolutely put the book to one side. I returned to the bag and was disappointed: the only other thing it contained was a blanket like the ones in the bunkers. So I picked up the bottle, which wasn't big, probably half a litre, full of a colourless liquid, like water, and had never been opened. I examined the cork at length and put off finding a way to open it until later. I was absolutely exhausted. The regular existence I led, walking for eight to ten hours every day in the wilderness, hadn't prepared me for this emotional upheaval. I was trembling with fatigue and I didn't even have the strength to make myself something to eat. I unfolded the blanket from the bag, stretched it out on the ground to air it and wrapped myself up in my own. I didn't even realise that I was falling asleep, and was amazed, on waking abruptly, to find it was three o'clock in the morning. I lit the fire and heated up some food. At sunrise,

I was back in the bus.

First, I took out all the kit bags and lined them up a few metres from the rusty shell of the bus, then I did likewise with the corpses. Reduced as they were to skeletons, they felt incredibly light. I was especially interested in their clothing. I wondered whether the lightweight cotton trousers and the shirt with epaulettes that I'd seen the guards in the bunker wearing would be more comfortable than my dress. One of the dead men had been small and slim and I decided to keep his clothes to try on after washing them. I put the weapons in two piles: the whips that would never crack again and the big pistols that they'd never drawn in the bunker, but whose use I had been told about. I was tempted to try them out, and took one, aimed and pulled the trigger. Nothing happened, and at the time, I told myself it was not loaded. Later, I remembered that those things had a safety catch and I thought that perhaps it had been on, but in any case, I wouldn't have known how to release it. Then I began searching all the bags and I wasn't surprised to find exactly the same in each one: a jacket, two pairs of under-pants, a packet of food—one, better preserved than the others, contained little whitish fragments which crumbled at my touch. I presumed it was bread, that everyday food which I had never eaten—a blanket, a razor and a book. I didn't even need to decipher the title to realise that they were all the same. I didn't dwell on the matter, fearing I'd experience anew the agitation that had defeated me the previous evening. Once I'd finished sorting everything out, I wondered why we'd never found any bread in any of the bunkers. I still have no idea.

By midday, everything was in order, the twenty-three skel-etons lying side by side, the shirts and underpants in neat piles, the masks and weapons in three separate heaps. I had examined the masks closely, and remembered stories told by the women:

they were probably gas masks. That made me wonder what had killed these men: certainly not gas, against which they had protection. Anyway, we'd escaped just minutes after the siren had stopped and nothing had happened to us.

I stood up and stretched. My back ached from bending over for so long, and I spent a long time examining my possessions before heating up my meal. Suddenly I was the owner of a vast number of goods, whereas I was used to owning nothing. I felt overwhelmed. I ate gazing at my skeletons. They'd been custodians of the absurd, carrying out orders whose purpose they were unaware of, themselves having to submit to incomprehensible rules, and perhaps they had no more idea of our identity than we did of theirs. Death had caught them unawares, sitting in the bus: but had they known where they were going? Since the siren, we'd never found any trace of the guards, and we imagined that they'd all been taken off somewhere else: why were these guards still here? The only possible explanations occurred to me much later: they were on a routine trip between two bunkers, they were on their way to sleep, or they might have been new arrivals being driven to their post, oblivious of the danger. The gas masks showed that this land was not safe, but whatever it was that killed them had been unforeseen. Ours was the only prison where the siren had sounded just as the cage door was opened, and that is what had saved us: they were the only ones who were exposed, and that had killed them. This symmetry preoccupied me for a long time. For some reason I found in it a sort of obscure beauty. Did something, someone, somewhere understand the meaning of all this? Were things still going on? And on this planet of which I will only ever see a fraction, however long I keep walking, was there a place where the bunkers were still operational? Where men and women obeyed the whip, slept and ate at random times, and where a rebellious girl was beginning to count her heartbeats? Was I the only one? Did the planet on which I was wandering have a thousand sister planets scattered across the starry sky and, at night, while I was waiting to fall asleep, and my gaze sometimes lit on some distant globe, was the same scene taking place there?

I decided to bury the skeletons, because I wanted to show that whatever had happened to us, we belonged to the same kind, to those who honour the dead. I dug twenty-three shallow graves and laid the skeletons in them, then I covered them with earth and made a little mound on top of each one, on which I placed the masks and the weapons. I arranged them in a circle, I don't know why, I felt that was best, their heads in the centre and their feet pointing towards the distance. It took me three days, because the ground was dry and I found it tiring. I rested by trying to decipher my books.

They were all carrying the same book: *A Condensed Gardening Handbook*. It explained how to plant, sow, thin out, hoe and weed, and what to do in which season and what to plant where. I read the entire book carefully and became an expert on grafting roses, which made me laugh. There were lots of illustrations which showed me what a hoe looked like, a tulip bulb and plenty of other things that I'd never seen and never would.

I read and reread the book. I acquired a perfectly useless knowledge, but I enjoyed it. I felt as if I had embellished my mind and that made me think of jewels, those objects which women used to adorn their beauty, in the days when beauty had a purpose.

By the fifth day, everything was in order. I'd chosen two pairs of trousers, two shirts, a jacket, several pairs of underpants, taken as many towels as possible and replaced the rest, neatly folded and wrapped in the blankets, on the seats of the bus. I repacked my rucksack, which was only a little heavier because I'd eaten the contents of many of the cans, when suddenly I spotted the bottles which I'd completely forgotten. Had I become so rich that I could neglect some of my possessions? I had to move on because my water supply was getting low and I needed to find a river or a bunker soon to replenish it, but I could take a little time to find out what was in the bottles. I had no implement to open them with, so I began digging out the cork with the tip of my knife, which was difficult and took a long time. At last, I was able to pour a little of the liquid into my cup. It smelled funny, very strong and not very pleasant to the nostrils. I dipped my finger in and licked it: I didn't like it. I took a tiny sip, which I swallowed gingerly, but even so it burnt my throat and made me want to cough. So it was alcohol, as I'd been expecting. At first, I was vexed, then I remembered that alcohol has medicinal qualities. In the past it had been used especially for cleaning wounds and numbing the senses when someone was in a great deal of pain. My wounds, nothing more serious than scratches on my legs when I brushed past thorn bushes, never became infected. All the same, it seemed like a good idea to take one bottle. I put the others back inside the bus.

Before departing, I gazed at the scene I was leaving behind: the rust-eaten bus, a shell in the middle of the plain, which, over the centuries, would slowly disintegrate where it stood, the tombs in a circle decorated with the masks and weapons, the silence barely disturbed by the constant whispering of the wind. It all seemed incredibly strange, sinister and moving. I felt the burden of the inexplicable, of my life, of that world to which I was the sole witness. I had nothing else to do in it but continue my journey. One day, I would die here. Like the guards.

I followed the road.

It hadn't been used for twenty years and, in places, despite the sparse vegetation, it was so overgrown that it disappeared and I had to climb a little hill to make out the bare strip. It took me in a south-west direction. I wondered whether it would lead to something. That would be logical, if there was any logic in this world. In the bus, two seats had remained empty: was the driver on his way to pick up three more guards, one of whom would have to stand, or was he driving the others to their final destination?

For three days, ten hours a day, I walked, once again spurred on by impatience. I'd stayed in one place for a long time and was reaching the end of my supplies when I saw a cabin. I went in, feeling no emotion, certain that I would only find, as usual, the lights on, the main doors open and the cage locked. In the cold store, I was glad to see a fairly small piece of lamb that would defrost and cook quite fast. Back at the top, I realised that I hadn't even glanced at the cage and its occupants. That made my heart sink, and I promised to go and pay my respects the next day.

That night, I had a dream that I remembered. In it, I was sitting inside the bus amid the guards, who were alive. I couldn't make out their faces because of the masks, but I could hear them talking among themselves. I had never actually heard the sound of a man's voice, but that didn't occur to me in my dream. The bus was moving. My situation felt completely natural, I didn't wonder where I was going, or what I was doing among the guards. This seemed to go on for ages and I was perfectly relaxed, surrounded by the men, when suddenly I rediscovered the exquisite eruption of before, when I used to make up stories that I kept to myself.

That woke me. I was alone, under my blanket, lying in

the middle of the plain, a few paces from the cabin. I felt an immense sadness on thinking that there had been men and their closeness could trigger that delicious tremor, but I was reduced, poor me! to encountering it by chance in a dream. For a few moments I wondered what gave me my determination to live. I thought of all those women who had been killed by despair well before they reached old age, of Laura who grew tired of keeping her soul tethered to her body, and I felt a sort of vague temptation, a gnawing urge to admit defeat, which terrified me. I got up and took a few steps. It was a clear night, the sky was vast, hill after hill, I had thousands of kilometres to cover. My curiosity, momentarily dampened, was reawakened.

The next day, I went back down the stairs and sat outside the cage. It was one of the few bunkers where the occupants had maintained their dignity to the end. There were no gruesome piles of twisted bodies, they were lying down, each on his own mattress, as if asleep. Perhaps one of them had had a powerful influence over the others and had convinced them that shouting and resistance would achieve nothing, that they had to resign themselves to dying and embrace their fate without putting up a futile struggle. Everything was in order, but, apart from bodies lying everywhere, how can you create disarray when you have nothing? I felt a sort of serenity looking at those corpses: they had died calmly and would spend eternity in tranquil postures. It set me wondering how I would die, whether it would be at night, in my sleep, and I would lie on the plain for ever, exposed to the constant gentle wind, or whether I would fall ill and have to endure pain. I remembered the guns, and then I remembered the safety catch, and told myself I should have persevered, I'd have been bound to find out how to use it, because I might end up wanting to die. I could have gone back to the bus, but I was extremely reluctant to retrace my steps when there was so much new ground ahead. I was young and healthy, and I had plenty of time to worry about that kind of precaution. Besides, I expected to make new discoveries. There had to be more than just cabins on that plain!

I filled one of the big cooking pots with water and boiled my washing for a long time on the guards' cooker. When it looked clean, I took it up and laid it out on the grass to dry in the sun. That took me the whole day.

I set off again. Now that I had a book and could learn to read, I was sorry not to have a pencil or anything else to write with, to make a note of my route. In the evening, before going to sleep, I practised writing letters in the dirt, copying the sentences and words from the book. I had used a lot of them in speech, so I recognised them, and I thought about how to construct those that were not in there. The first one I tried to spell was 'cabin': I had 'ca' from 'can' and 'bin' from 'compost bin'—I just had to put the two together to make 'cabin'. Then I spelled 'cage'. The magic 'e' made the 'a' say its own name, unlike the short 'a' in 'cabin'. I felt very pleased with myself for working this out and it looked as though I remembered everything I'd been taught.

Sometimes, busying myself in this way, I automatically spoke the words I was trying to write and I was astonished at the sound of my voice, which had become cracked and raucous. I was probably forgetting how to talk through lack of practice. That worried me a little, then I shrugged: so what if I completely forgot how to speak? I would never talk to anyone again!

All the same, I felt nostalgic for a moment. That wonderful dream never recurred, and I was sometimes acutely aware that I was alone, and always would be, and that the only pleasure within my grasp was the all-too-rare one of satisfied curiosity.

I continued from bunker to bunker. In so far as there

were seasons on this planet where things varied so little, winter returned. The temperature was slightly cooler and it often rained during the night. I slept wrapped in the waterproof sheet and I set out a little later in the morning, as I had to wait for it to dry. I wore trousers and the jacket. While waiting for better weather, when I wasn't working on my reading, I made myself a dress from the towels. The ground became greener and the streams deeper. I lost the road.

It had become harder and harder to follow. At first, I told myself I must have made a mistake and confused it with the natural formation of the land. Much as I disliked doing so, I retraced my steps. I thought I'd found it again at the top of a hill, and I scanned the countryside carefully. The direction I'd come from seemed to be the right one, so I went back the same way, hoping that I'd only missed it through a lapse of concentration. I waited for the low evening sunlight, which emphasised the contours of the landscape, and I saw the thin ribbon stretching up the hill opposite. At dawn the next day, I was able to make out further clues, but after an hour's walking, I could no longer see any clear signs. I decided to cover a vast semicircular area with a radius of five thousand steps. For three days, I walked back and forth, and had to resign myself to the fact that the road ended there.

I was bitterly disappointed. I had so hoped that it would lead me somewhere, I'd forgotten that nothing made sense in that wilderness. Do people build roads that suddenly vanish? Yes, I told myself, yes, those people did. I felt like sitting down on the ground and weeping, but, luckily, my anger was the stronger and drove me on. I had to decide on a new direction. At first I'd chosen the east, then the road had made me deviate towards the south-west, and now I resolved to go due south.

I had less energy. The road and the bus, which had given

me so much hope, had turned out to be insoluble mysteries like everything else, and from time to time I said to myself that it was a pretty meagre reward after two years' walking. But gradually my natural resilience took over again and, as I made my way from one hilltop to another, it occurred to me to organise my route more cleverly than in a straight line. By going straight, I was only exploring a very narrow area, and perhaps I was missing things to the left or right. The fruitless semicircle gave me an idea: I would walk in huge parallel arcs, two or three hours' apart, depending on how I felt, and on the appeal of the terrain. Of course, that was much harder to calculate than going straight ahead, when all I had to do was pick out the landmarks and walk towards them. I knew that if you followed the sun, you'd go round in a circle. I got involved in complicated reckonings and experiments on the ground: I needed to follow the sun for a while and then change direction at midday. At that time, I had no means of making a map of my journey, but in the evenings, I drew it on the ground with stones and gazed at it for a long time to ensure I had memorised it. I began to wonder whether the bunkers were dotted around at random, or whether their location was governed by a plan. On our first exploratory trip, it had been twenty-six days before we'd found one, but sometimes I walked for barely a week before being able to stock up afresh. I walked in several semicircles, then, when I was certain I could orientate myself, I made big zigzags along the arcs of the circle: after a few weeks, I realised that the bunkers were arranged in groups of five, one at each corner of a rectangle and one in the centre. By keeping to a straight line, naturally, I missed some. I soon became able, on arriving at a cabin, to work out which way to go to find the next one, and could go to them or avoid them as I chose. I never avoided them and, whether I needed food or not, I'd go down to pay my respects to the dead. I never came across an open prison door.

The coincidence that had made the siren go off at the precise moment when the guard was putting his key in the lock had been unique. Sometimes I marvel at my fate: I had been the only child among the women, and we were the prisoners who had escaped with our lives. For a few years.

This new control over my route dispelled my melancholy mood. After all, I had made one discovery, so why had I allowed it to make me depressed? There would be more.

I made another discovery.

It was at the end of the day. I was tired and was looking for a patch of ground that would be a good place to stop. It had rained for several nights, but that evening the sky was cloudless, so I could rely on dry weather, which was a relief because I hadn't been able to light a fire and had eaten my canned food cold and congealed. In other words, I needed a thick grove where I'd find plenty of wood to cut, with as few brambles as possible. I looked carefully about me, but with a specific objective, which nearly caused me to miss the mound of stones. I'd almost gone past it when the feeling of something unusual made me stop. I turned round and saw the mound that stood out so sharply against the monotony of the plain. There were never piles! It was two metres wide and reached almost to my knees. I'd never encountered anything like it—at most, I'd seen a few large stones close to each other, but what I found here couldn't be natural. I took off my rucksack, put it slowly down on the ground and caught my breath.

I was almost afraid to start moving the stones. I had to rouse myself. The stones were fairly large and I could only pick up one at a time. I realised that I was likely to graze my palms, so I tore off a strip from the blanket and wrapped it around my hands, which slowed me down, but in a way, I found it a relief.

I was terribly afraid of being disappointed and finding, after all that effort, nothing but a few shade-loving insects. The pile was artificial, there was absolutely no doubt about that. If it concealed nothing, I would have to ask myself why someone had made it and all I'd have gained would be a new question, that worthless treasure which was beginning to weary me. This world was like a jigsaw puzzle, I only had a few pieces which didn't fit together. Once, Anthea had explained that game to me and it sounded as though I'd have enjoyed it.

I concentrated on removing the stones evenly from the top of the pile to avoid a rock slide. It was slow work and it took me more than an hour to reach the last layer of stones, which were much smaller and in the shape of a circle. I took the shovel I used every evening to level the ground and began to scrape the earth carefully. I was on my knees, like the pilgrims of the past, and certainly trembling like one. The shovel soon struck a metal surface.

My whole being leapt! An intense tremor rippled through me and I felt giddy. I stood still for a few moments, regaining my breath, stunned and almost afraid. I put down the shovel and bandaged my hands again to remove the last stones. Drops of perspiration fell from my forehead and I was quaking with impatience, but I continued to work slowly and methodically. Within three minutes, everything was clear: in front of me was a round metal cover, a metre in diameter, with a slightly rusty handle set off-centre. I picked up a screwdriver to free and raise it. Was I going to have to lift this heavy-looking plate? I was confused and almost in despair, telling myself that I probably wouldn't have the strength, but I tugged at the handle just in case. I felt something move, I tugged again and found that the plate rotated on a horizontal axis, stiffly, and with a scraping sound, but it required no more strength than I had. It rose up,

surrounded by a rim of steel, and I saw, at a depth of half a
metre, a small ledge on which I could stand. I lowered myself
in gingerly, my hands on the edges. As soon as I'd gained a
foothold, I realised I was on the top step of a very narrow spiral
staircase that was unlit. At that time, I'd never experienced the
profound darkness of enclosed spaces, because the light never
went out in the bunkers, but the women had spoken of switches.
I felt along the wall. They hadn't given a precise description,
but I thought they must be small objects positioned near doors.
I began groping my way down the stairs, and when I reached
the third step I felt something small and smooth with a button.
I pressed: a big light came on, just at my feet. The wall was
grey and rough like the walls in the bunkers, but the staircases
were never spiral like this, and you couldn't control the light. I
continued my descent, hurrying at first, but I think I'd only got
to about the tenth step when I started feeling dizzy. I stopped,
and, despite my impatience, forced myself to wait a few minutes until the giddiness had passed. As soon as I started moving
again, it returned. Later, I was able to run up and down it, but
that first time, even though I was consumed with curiosity, I
had to stop several times. There were eighty open-work metal
steps. At last I saw the floor, made of the same rough material as
the walls. One last turn and I was at the bottom, in a corridor
that was six or seven paces wide and twelve paces long, lined
from top to bottom with shelves laden with cans, bottles and
packets of all kinds, and closed at the end by a door of a very
strange material that I had never seen before. It opened easily
to reveal a big square room, which wasn't grey and gloomy
like the bunkers. The walls were entirely covered in a beautiful
wood with a dark sheen, and the floor was soft underfoot. I
understood that, for the first time in my life, I was about to walk
on carpet. Lamps at various points in the room gave off a warm

glow, which fell in brighter puddles on a big table, and there were wide, low chairs which I recognised at once as the kind of object that used to be called armchairs. I was choked with admiration. I'd never seen anything so beautiful, because I'd never seen anything beautiful that was the work of a human hand. I had seen the beauty of the sky, the changing shapes of the clouds, softly falling rain; I had seen the slowly moving stars, and a few flowers, but here, I was seeing furniture, paintings hanging on the walls, vases, a small carving—but I shouldn't be describing these things so precisely, because that first moment I saw only the interplay of lines, shapes and harmonious colours, an unfathomable configuration that completely overwhelmed me, and brought tears to my eyes because of the feeling of calm and tranquillity that reminded me of the women's singing, in the past, when it rose up over the plain. The colours were beautifully in tune with each other, and harmonised with the volumes and dimensions of the room. I was still giddy from the descent, and I crouched down because I felt as though I might fall over. After a few minutes, I thought it would be a good idea to close my eyes, the giddiness hadn't gone but was even getting worse. I rested my head on my folded arms. I breathed deeply and did something I hadn't done for years, I began counting my heartbeats. This recourse to a very old habit seemed to soothe me. All the same, more than an hour went by before I could calmly begin exploring my new kingdom. I tried several times to raise my head and open my eyes, but I was immediately overcome with emotion, I had to curl up in a ball again and wait, patiently, for the storm to subside.

I was confronted with the human past, in a place that had been designed for the pleasure of the person who would live there. It was completely different from the bunkers. I had only known the prisons, the instruments that served basic needs, the whips and straw mattresses that had to be piled up so we could move around. But this secret underground place was a home.

I have never changed anything in the way this room is arranged; each time I use an object, I put it back in exactly the same place. There were three chairs on either side of the table on which stood a lamp with a beautiful ochre lampshade, and a large clear glass dish. Away from the table, there were three armchairs around another, lower table, and a big bed with a colourful bed-spread on which several cushions were casually scattered. When I was able to look around, I saw, on my right, what must have been the kitchen, with a sink, hotplates and a cupboard containing saucepans and white china plates with a blue floral pattern. One of the taps provided hot water, and the other cold. To the left of the sink was a door unlike anything I'd ever seen, a single wooden door painted white, which opened into a much smaller room, with a toilet, a washbasin and a bathtub.

When I'd inspected everything, I sat down on one of the chairs, and then in an armchair. I began to laugh. It had taken more than two hours for my amazement and emotion to turn to joy.

There was so much to investigate and taking it all in was so thrilling that I hadn't yet realised that one of the ornaments on the wall was a shelf laden with books. My head started spinning again, and I stood staring across the room at them for ages. I had read and reread my gardening manual and knew it by heart. I could feel my eyes widening before this gift, and, to get over the shock, I began to count: there were nineteen books, eight of which were very fat, about three fingers wide. I went over to them: their titles were printed on the spines. At first, I was so intimidated that I tried to decipher them from a dis-tance and thought I'd forgotten how to read. I raised my hand and took one—it felt surprisingly heavy—then I sat down and stood it up on its edge. On it was written: *Elementary Treatise on Astronautics*. I opened it. The pages were full of words and strange signs among which I recognised the few symbols that Anthea had taught me: plus, minus, multiply by, divide by and equals. I think it was only fatigue that made me wise enough not to go any further that evening. Afterwards, I discovered that some of the others were more in-depth studies on the same subject. I have read them all, every single word. I didn't understand a thing.

Do I understand Shakespeare's plays any better, or the story of Don Quixote de la Mancha, or what is going on in Dostoevsky's novels? I think not. They all speak of experiences that I have not known. I think I do better with objects—it took me hours to work out how to use a corkscrew and open a bottle of wine, but I managed it. Feelings remain a mystery to me, perhaps because the sensations associated with them are foreign to me, or because they repel me as did physical contact, which seems to be so important in love. Whenever I think of Anthea's death and the effort it took to hold her in my arms, tears come into my eyes. I try to imagine myself being warm: there's always a point when the whip cracks. A lot of things the women used to tell me about still puzzle me: I know that there used to be such a thing as money, that everything had to be bought and that they always found it strange to go and stock up from the cold stores without having to pay anyone, but it all remained rather abstract and I can't really understand why people kill for money like poor old Raskolnikov. True, I have killed, but I did so to relieve my companions' suffering, and I always had the impression that they were grateful to me. But perhaps I shouldn't be so certain: my ignorance of human feelings is so vast that they might have hated me without my being aware of it. Nor do I understand why it is humiliating to wear second-hand clothing—I have rarely worn anything else!

I loved Rose's songs and I expect I'd have appreciated music more than literature. If there are recordings in this place and the equipment to play them, I haven't identified them.

I realised that five hours had gone by since, up above, I had felt tired and decided to stop, then noticed the mound of stones. I was hungry. I opened one of the cans and ate the contents cold. I assumed that the hotplates were working perfectly, like the lamps, but I'd had enough shocks. I was exhausted and didn't even want to try them. I unfolded my blanket and laid it on the carpet, putting off using the bed until later. After the whirlwind of emotions, I thought I'd sleep for a long time, but the excitement was too much and after three hours, I woke with a start and was starving again. I went into the kitchen and boiled some water in a pretty little saucepan. The door of the cold store was to the right of the sink, and I was amazed to find a room that was even bigger than the one in the bunkers, crammed to the ceiling with all sorts of meats, but also vegetables and fruit. Each bag had been carefully labelled: there were foods that I'd heard of, but which weren't to be found in the bunkers, like chicken, venison and roebuck, powdered eggs, tomatoes, parsley, cheese and hundreds of other delicacies which I've since become familiar with. And bread, which delighted me especially. I decided to have a party, with a chicken which I sprinkled with herbs, tomatoes, potato croquettes and strawberry jam spread on bread and butter. I put everything out to defrost in the kitchen. Later, I found out how to use a sort of oven in which you can reheat food in a few seconds, but that time, I had to wait several hours. I was so busy that the time flew by. I ran a scalding bath and for the first time I experienced the luxury that the women had so missed. Later, it became something quite mundane and it was only on my return from expeditions that I rediscovered the magic of immersing myself in deliciously hot water in which I liked to fall asleep. There were bars of soap. Of course, every-thing was new to me and required long periods of thought: the soap bar had me baffled. I was amazed by its scent, which was so unusual for me who had known no other smells than those of the grasses, the few wild flowers and the earth after the rain. I tasted it and pulled a face, it was certainly not something to eat, then I recalled things the women had told me and I rubbed it on my hands, but that was no use, because I hadn't realised that you had to wet them first. In the end, I got there and I used soap to wash my hair. When it was dry, I was amazed to find my hair so light and flowing, framing my face so graciously.

I nearly forgot! Of course, one of the most wonderful discoveries was the mirror. I had never seen myself. Anthea had told me I was pretty, but that meant nothing to me, and still didn't. Even so, I was fascinated and spent hours gazing at myself. I didn't know my expressions; I learned what my smile looked like, and my serious or worried look, and I stared at them thinking: 'That's me.'

Even now, I like to look in the mirror. Over the years, I've followed the progress of the wrinkles furrowing my brow. My cheeks have grown thinner and my lips have become pale, but it's all me and I feel a sort of fondness for the reflection in the mirror. I must have been fourteen or fifteen when we got out, and Laura had died twenty-three years later. I'd walked for two years before arriving here, in this place which I call my home: so then I was just over forty. That was twenty-two years ago. I suppose I am an old woman, but I still love looking at my face. I don't know if it's beautiful or ugly, but it is the only human face I ever see. I smile at it and receive a friendly smile back.

I opened the cupboards in the bathroom and found a pile of towels, but nothing else. I presumed they were awaiting the baggage of the occupant who'd never arrived. There was nothing put there in advance, which was a pity as it would have told me something about him.

Then I went back into the kitchen, made some white coffee and put some egg powder in water to make an omelette according to the instructions on the packet. Then, I pulled back the bed covers and slept with my head on a pillow for the first time in my life. I liked that very much.

The next day, I began my inventory of the corridor. It contained various tools and a number of objects whose use I never did fathom. I suppose they're electrical gadgets, perhaps assembled, perhaps in parts. The women had talked of radios, televisions, telephones, motorcycles and cars, and the books on astronautics made me wonder whether it was laboratory equipment that had not found its destined use. There were no written instructions except for the defrosting oven in the kitchen, thanks to which I was able to learn to use it. I prowled around the equipment in the corridor for ages, picking it up and putting it back, because I knew full well that my determination wouldn't make up for the information I lacked. I still go and look at it sometimes. After all, I didn't really know how to read when I found the gardening manual, but I managed to decipher it. I can count well, I can add and subtract easily, but I still find multiplication and division difficult. According to Anthea, that's because I didn't learn my multiplication tables until I was quite old, and you need to learn them when you're very young for them to be etched in your mind. Other than that, I know nothing, and the objects in the corridor come from a sophisticated technological civilisation of which I haven't the least idea. The women had taught me what they knew, which was little— they'd forgotten a lot and, besides, they lacked the implements to show me things. So, I know that people used to knit, and we could have made knitting needles by smoothing very straight twigs, but we didn't have any wool. I sew when I find thread, which isn't often. There was none in the house. With time, I completely wore out my trousers and shirts, but I found a nice piece of fabric in a bunker and I'm wearing tunics again.

The most precious thing I found in the bunker is paper. There were several reams, and a box of pencils. That was how I was at last able to learn to write. The books helped me, even the ones on astronautics. Admittedly, I didn't understand the mathematics, but they contained many lengthy chapters of explanations in which I studied the ways of saying things, the spelling and the grammar. I spent a lot of time studying the incomprehensible diagrams which went with the text. I copied them and that taught me to draw accurately, keeping the proportions right, so that I was able to map my excursions.

I decided that this bunker would be my home base. I asked myself hundreds of questions about its purpose. It wasn't marked by a cabin, but by a mound of stones that could easily be overlooked, and I wondered whether they were meant to conceal it or mark it. It contained more provisions than I'd ever seen in the prisons, and I'd be able to live there for ever. It seemed to me that it was a luxurious place, but obviously I didn't have a clear idea of luxury. In the ceiling, there are the same air-conditioning grates as in the other bunkers and, when I keep absolutely quiet, I can hear the same soft hum that indicates that everything is working. The bed is very big, several people could sleep in it, and there's room for six people to sit around the table. In the kitchen there are four dozen glasses and several different kinds of plate. Does one person need all that? I am really sorry that there are no clothes, for not only would it have been useful to find some, but I could also have learned a lot from them. The books only taught me to write. Was this the home of a leader or an outlaw's hideout? I am certainly too ignorant to interpret things that would probably have been blindingly clear to the women with whom I'd lived, for they at least had seen the world.

Then I gave up asking pointless questions. I examined everything, but I knew no more about the absent owner of my home than I had done on my arrival. I no longer think about him. Whatever his plans had been, he failed and his domain was now mine. Neither he nor I can do anything about that.

After two months, I set off exploring again. I made more than fifty expeditions, either walking in straight lines or in concentric semicircles. I found nothing but locked prisons. Perhaps there were other places like the one where I'd made my home, but I didn't see them, even though I never forgot to inspect the ground, patiently looking for another mound of stones. I have understood nothing about the world in which I live. I have criss-crossed it in every direction but I haven't discovered its boundaries.

On my last trip, I was standing on top of a hill, before me stretched a long walk down and a new plain and I could see a cabin in the distance. Suddenly, I was overcome with despondency. I told myself another staircase, the guards' room, the cage and forty emaciated corpses. I sat down and the realisation dawned on me that I'd had enough. For the twenty or so years that I'd been alone, hope had buoyed me up, and suddenly, it had deserted me. I had imagined, a thousand times, a bunker where the cage would be open, where the prisoners, intoxicated with joy could have escaped. They'd have found the sky, the plain, they'd have trembled, dreamed of towns, of rescuers, but would, like us, have discovered this same hollow freedom. It was as if I could see them before me, looking at me and demanding an explanation: is this what you have to offer us? Leave us alone, we're better off dead than desperate. I bowed my head and set off home.

Yet, I set about writing this account: apparently, even if I no longer have the strength or the heart to go off exploring again, my hope, which waned briefly, has not really expired. The bunker I didn't enter might have been the one, or the next one, or another one to the west that time I went east. Who knows whether, one day, a very old man or a very old woman might arrive here, see the raised cover, be amazed, hope, and start descending the spiral staircase? That person will find these sheets of paper piled on the big wooden table and read them, and someone will at last receive a message from another person. Perhaps, at this very moment, as I end my days exhausted, a human being is walking across the plain as I did, going from bunker to bunker, a rucksack on their back, determinedly seeking an answer to the thousands of questions consuming them. I know that I can't wait much longer, that I will soon have to deal myself the death blow that my companions so often requested, because the pain is becoming increasingly relentless.

From time to time, at night, I go upstairs and sit outside. I listen. Recently, I resolved to try and shout at the top of my voice: 'Hello! Is anybody there?' My voice was croaky and weak, but I still listened. I heard only the soft rustle of the grass in the breeze. Another time, I collected lots of branches and made a fire that could be seen from a long way off. I kept it going all night, although my common sense told me that there was no one. But it also told me that there are so many bunkers and that probably, most probably, there was another one where the siren had gone off when the door was open, and why should they all be dead? The night goes by, I think of my life, the girl in a rage who taunted the young guard, angry at the present—as if I had a future—or easily climbing the hundred stairs, caught in the web of illusions in the middle of the boundless desolate plain, under a sky that is nearly always grey, or such a pale blue that it seems to be dying. But a sky does not die, it is I who am dying, who was already dying in the bunker—and I tell myself that I am alone in this land that no longer has any jailers, or prisoners, unaware of what I came here to do, the mistress of silence, owner of bunkers and corpses. I tell myself that I have walked for thousands of hours and that soon I will take my last ten steps to go and put these sheets of paper on the table and come back to lie down on my deathbed, an emaciated old woman whose eyes, which no hand will close, will always be looking towards the door. I have spent my whole life doing I don't know what, but it hasn't made me happy. I have a few drops of blood left, that is the only libation I can offer destiny, which has chosen me. Then I see the pale winter dawn break and I go back down to sleep, if the pain allows me any respite, on the big bed where there is room for several people.

There is always light. Sometimes I hope that one night it will go out, that something will happen. The women were always wondering where it came from. I never really understood their explanations of power stations, pylons, conductor wires, and I have never seen anything corresponding to their hazy descriptions. I have seen only the plain, the cabins, and the shelter where I am ending my days. I have long since stopped trying to imagine things I do not know. I have spent a lot of time studying the objects on the shelves in the corridor, but I have learned nothing. They are perhaps weapons, or a means of communication that would have enabled me to contact humanity. Too bad. I gave up reading and rereading the books and treatises on astronautics. So few things happened during all those years of walking. I found the bus, I lost the road, I arrived here. In any case, I had to die some day. Even if I'd led a normal life, like the women before, I would still have found myself at the dawn of my last day. Sometimes the women pitied me, saying that at least they'd known real life, and I was very jealous of them, but they died, as I am about to die, and what does having lived mean once you are no longer alive? If I hadn't fallen ill, I think I'd have set off again all the same, and would still be walking, because I have never had anything else to do.

I know, even when I pretend the contrary, that I am the only living person on this planet which has almost no seasons. Only I can say that time exists, but it has passed me by without my feeling it. I saw the other women grow old. I go over to the mirror and look at myself: I suppose I didn't use to have those lines across my cheeks and around my eyes, but I don't remember my face before the wrinkles. The women had explained to me what photos were, but I don't have any. All I know about time is that the days follow on from one another, I feel tired and I sleep, I feel hungry and I eat. Of course, I count. Every thirty days, I say to myself that a month has gone by, but those are mere words, they don't really give me time. Perhaps you never have time when you are alone? You only acquire it by watching it go by in others, and since all the women have died, it only affects the scrawny plants growing between the stones and producing, occasionally, just enough flowers to make a single seed which will fall a little way off—not far because the wind is never strong—where it may or may not germinate. The alternation of day and night is merely a physical phenomenon, time is a question of being human and, frankly, how could I consider myself a human being, I who have only known thirty-nine people and all of them women? I think that time must have something to do with the duration of pregnancies, the growth of children, all those things that I haven't experienced. If someone spoke to me, there would be time, the beginning and end of what they said to me, the moment when I answered, their response. The briefest conversation creates time. Perhaps I have tried to create time through writing these pages. I begin, I fill them with words, I pile them up, and I still don't exist because nobody is reading them. I am writing them for some unknown reader who will probably never come—I am not even sure that humanity has survived that mysterious event that governed my life. But if that person comes, they will read them and I will have a time in their mind. They will have my thoughts in them. The reader and I thus mingled will constitute something living, that will not be me, because I will be dead, and will not be that person as they were before reading, because my story, added to their mind, will then become part of their thinking. I will only be truly dead if nobody ever comes, if the centuries, then the millennia go by for so long that this planet, which I no longer believe is Earth, no longer exists. As long as the sheets of paper covered in my handwriting lie on this table, I can become a reality in someone's mind. Then everything will be obliterated, the suns will burn out and I will disappear like the universe.

Most likely no one will come. I shall leave the door open and my story on the table, where it will gradually gather dust. One day, the natural cataclysms that destroy planets will wipe out the plain, the shelter will collapse on top of the little pile of neatly arranged pages, they will be scattered among the debris, never read.

I found out I was ill three months ago. I was on the toilet, passing a motion, when I experienced a new sensation: something warm was trickling down my vagina, that part of my body which had always been so silent that I never thought about its existence. I leaned over the bowl and saw a big black clot, with yellowish filaments. Before I had a chance to panic, I lost a stream of blood, and the pain was so acute that I passed out. When I came to, I was lying on the floor, and it no longer hurt. I got up without too much difficulty, I felt a little giddy, perhaps because of the haemorrhage, but it quickly wore off. I washed, then I cleaned the bloodstained floor, and, remembering what Anthea had taught me, I grilled a piece of red meat to make up for the loss.

The women had talked of the menopause, but I don't suppose that it affected me, because I'd never reached puberty. However, there's no reason to suppose that I don't have a uterus, or ovaries, even if they haven't developed normally. I was puzzled, then I told myself that there was no point worrying and tried to forget the incident. I'm not adept at this kind of mental activity, and even if I had been, it would not have served me for long. The same thing happened the following day. My symptoms were similar to those of Mary-Jane, who according to Anthea, had a cancer of the sexual organs and went and hanged herself from the bars when she could no longer stand the pain. There was no other alternative, and I wouldn't receive any different treatment. Anthea had told me that they performed operations, gave morphine. Perhaps there are medicines in the corridor, but I am unable to identify them, and I've never found anything that looks like those bottles from which the guards sometimes took white pills when someone had a temperature.

The pain has been excruciating from the beginning, and it is becoming too frequent. I am suffering more than half the time, it takes away all pleasure from life and I'm unable to enjoy the moments of respite because I am so weak. I can no longer climb the stairs in one go and, when I get to the top, I am cold. After a quarter of an hour's walk, I have to rest. Probably the fact that I no longer eat much doesn't help, but if I force myself, I feel nauseous. I am nearing my end.

I am all alone. Even though I sometimes dream of a visitor, I have walked backwards and forwards over the plain for too long to believe it possible. No one will come because there are only corpses. How could the father of Prince Hamlet, if he was dead, appear and talk to him? The dead cannot move, they decompose on the spot and are eventually reduced to bones that will crumble at the slightest touch. I have seen hundreds, and none of them has ever come and talked to me in the middle of the night. I would have been so happy if they had! Anthea had tried to explain to me what the Christians meant by God, and the soul. Apparently, people believed firmly in it, it's even mentioned in the preface to one of the books on astronautics. Sometimes, I used to sit under the sky, on a clear night, and gaze at the stars, saying, in my croaky voice: 'Lord, if you're up there somewhere, and you aren't too busy, come and say a few words to me, because I'm very lonely and it would make me so happy.' Nothing happened. So I reckon that humanity—which I wonder whether I belong to—really had a very vivid imagination.

I can't be very old: if I left the bunker at around fifteen, I'm not much over sixty. The women said that, in the other world, life expectancy was more than seventy. But it required medical care. There, I'd have had periods and children, and my useless womb wouldn't have rotted. I often have haemorrhages, my womb is disintegrating, I know better than to hope that one day it will be reduced to nothing and I'll regain my health. For some time I have been coughing and I have chest pains: Anthea had told me about metastasis. In any case, it would soon be time to take a hand, but I shan't wait, I will do it in a little while, because I have almost finished my story and, after the final full stop, there will be nothing to hold me back.

As soon as I realised I was ill, I thought about ways of killing myself. I don't want to hang myself and dangle mummified on the end of a rope for ever. I want to be lying with dignity, like the man sitting between the folded mattresses; I want to be looking straight ahead of me, but if the pain is too great, I risk something unpleasant. I don't have either enough time or strength left to go to the bus and retrieve one of the guns that I placed on the tombs, so I sharpened a knife for a long time. If I brush my finger against it, I cut myself. The blade is thin, flat and sturdy. I know where to plunge it so that it goes in straight between two ribs, pierces my heart and stops it. When the pain leaves me in peace, I find it hard to believe that I will do it, when it rampages, my doubts vanish.

I will sit on the bed, and arrange the cushions and blankets rolled up around me so that my body is firmly supported. Everything will be perfectly clean and tidy. I hope there'll be no blood, which I know is possible. Perhaps nobody will ever come, perhaps one day, an astounded human being, arriving at the foot of the stairs as I did so long ago, will see the dark wood-panelled room, the neatly arranged bed, and an old woman sitting upright, a knife in her heart, looking peaceful.

It is strange that I am dying from a diseased womb, I who have never had periods and who have never known men.

AFTERWORD

Sometimes we read a book of such singularity and uniqueness, yet such ringing truth, that we wonder why it has not found a larger audience. Jacqueline Harpman's *I Who Have Never Known Men* is beloved by a small and intense core of readers, and yet has not entered mainstream awareness. Perhaps that's not so surprising, refusing as it does to be put into a neat genre box. It's a philosophical treatise as much as it is a story about an alien world, one that prizes the humanity of its characters and places this humanity square, front and centre, even in a disorientating landscape of total strangeness. The prose is cool water. Its images are lonely, weird, sometimes horrific, and always arresting.

In recent years we have seen a boom in science and speculative fiction written by female authors, but *I Who Have Never Known Men* seems eerily prescient, a book from a hundred years ago or a hundred years in the future. Lumping together female-centred science fiction can be reductive; problems of women are still problems that affect everyone living under patriarchy. In fact, femaleness is somehow both central to and almost incidental in this novel. Yes, there are men among the dead, but the novel would look very different were men to make an appearance beyond their roles as guards and dead prisoners.

The narrator is at the heart of this doubleness, presenting her memories and theories to us from a space of peculiar neutrality. She is not like the other women of the novel, with their memories of the outside world and knowledge of relationships, sex, love and family. Her body never developed the markers of reproduction, and being raised in an underground bunker since an early age, she is in a unique position to be a person without any of the signifiers of personhood. She is an example of a person raised without culture, without societal constructs, without knowledge. She is a pure experiment asking: what does a person become when stripped to the core, raised in isolation? What might a woman be like under these conditions? It is testament to the strength and beauty of this novel that she remains a character too, not just a device; she is formed, sympathetic, and possessing both curiosity and courage.

Nowhere in this novel is exploitation, pain for the sake of pain, or needless cruelty. The entire novel manages to balance its elegant philosophical concerns with also being an amazing feat of human tenderness. Everything is pared down, and everything has a purpose. Harpman shows the worst of what humans can inflict on humans, but also the best that love and togetherness can do. It is a 'minute account of a nightmare' (Hector Bianciotti, *Le Monde*) and yet also a triumph of the small, seemingly trivial fragments that make up who we are. 'It's all so ordinary, it's the same as everybody else!' exclaims one of the women when talking about her previous life; to which the narrator responds with 'As if she did not realise that for me, nothing was ordinary, since nothing had happened to me'.

No life is ordinary, the book seems to say. No life is without hope, without light, even during the unimaginable.

The plot of *I Who Have Never Known Men* is simple. Forty women are held in what appears to be an underground bunker, where they have been for many years. They are controlled by male guards, and the usual basic provisions of modernity—electricity, food, water—are available to them. Life continues for many years, until one day a siren goes off. By a stroke of luck the women are able to free themselves, and they start out upon a mysterious world gradually realising, horror after horror, that they might be the last people on this alien-seeming planet.

Despite this the novel chooses to begin with life—focusing on the narrator's coming of age, as shown through her fascination with the youngest male guard. The narrator gives us a frank description of her own burgeoning sexuality, while simultaneously remaining dislocated from it. In many ways she is as much an alien as the planet she lives on, compared to the other women, who spent their lives working service jobs and raising families. She has no idea of what a 'normal' human life might look like, and the other women react to this with unease.

But maybe it is femininity itself that is the strange thing. From the offing the narrator's sexual fascination with the guard calls up modern echoes of submissiveness and fantasy. What could be more human than want and desire: the machinations of your body kicking in? (And what a strange thing we are forced to admit desire is, when seen at this distance.) The narrator observes human behaviour and bodies objectively, in a way that is both curious and dehumanising; her perspective emphasises both her disconnection with her body, and the essential strangeness of having one, particularly one that you have not been taught about, one controlled by others. She may not have the learned behaviours of dances and marriages, but even a person raised in captivity learns to want, yearns to see beyond their cage.

How much of our humanity is intrinsic? How much remains, when all else is stripped away?

The story and the world the novel takes place in is pared down to the point of frustration. It possesses a Daliesque surrealism; its landscape owes as much to Beckett as it does to Bradbury. The world the liberated women walk through seems desolate, dotted from time to time with trees, rivers, and nightmare bunkers just like the one they have escaped from. There is no sense of who has confined them and for what reason, whether they're even wandering Earth. The sparse clues muddy the water further: unchanging seasons, a bus full of dead guards, captives in cages, a luxurious bunker underground. Nothing is explained, but nothing needs to be. The beauty and power of the novel is in its ambiguities, in the hypotheticals allowed to flourish and demonstrate what they need to demonstrate. It should be unremittingly bleak, for all the ingredients for bleakness are there; and yet there is a shining, searching humanity at its core that carries it through.

As the narrator discovers her own sense of selfhood and agency, the older women cling on to theirs: they discuss their pasts, they rail against having to use the toilet in front of everybody else, they discuss recipes when cooking their meagre rations of meat, water and potatoes. They are aware that the narrator exists in a different world to them, that she is of this world in a way that they are not, a bridging person between the old order and the new. Later on, devastatingly and compassionately, it is this difference that enables the narrator to enact fatal acts of love upon the older women. Death, in this world, has its own dignity, a dignity repeatedly exhorted as human. The other caged humans they discover have died terrible deaths, but the narrator admires those who have died calmly, facing the terror, unafraid. It is human to be afraid of death, of unimaginable pain, and it's another kind of humanity to transcend it.

This approach to death, to suffering, makes it difficult to analyse such a novel without acknowledging that the author was Jewish, having fled to Casablanca with her family during the Second World War. There are echoes of concentration camps in the senseless cruelty of their confinement, the endless cracking of the whips of the mysterious prison guards, the sickening inevitability as they discover, over and over and over, that everyone else on the planet imprisoned in the same way as them has perished. And for what? A project with a vague beginning—the 'confusion' the women allude to, sirens and fire and being taken from their homes—and then nothing but an endless, pointless confinement.

Forty women in a cage; a freezer full of food at temperatures low enough to last indefinitely; electricity and water that never ceases. These situations of confinement, of cruelty, of hopelessness, are not without precedent—we're kidding ourselves if we think of these cruelties as ones unique to a fictional alien planet.

But there is love, as well as horror, all the way through the novel. The quiet not-quite-utopia—the best that they can manage, given the strange world, their isolation—recalls a subverted *Herland* by Charlotte Perkins Gilman. It is a peaceful world they create, one where they stop searching, where they build houses and settle into routines and pair into couples. They form the best possible utopia available to them, despite all the odds, and so they live out their lives that way, despite the unimaginable trauma laid upon them for years. While they mourn the absence of men at least a little, particularly at the start, they also manage very well without them. The only man dwelled upon at any length in the novel is the youngest prison guard, and only in the context of the narrator's physical reaction to him.

Though this utopia is one without hope of their discovery, or the possibility that they might learn more about their condition, it is one where the characters can live out their days. The women can continue to find a sort of beauty in companionship, adapting to a new way of being, existing in an environment empty of what they know but still underpinned by compassion. But it's not necessarily extolling this kind of existence. Perhaps in its own way the novel slyly demonstrates the natural peacefulness that a world without men might possess, but also suggests that this settling is the downfall of the women, that they do not go on searching. Would they have searched further, railed more, had men been part of their party? Would they have found the answers over a distant horizon, even if decades in the future?

I love this book; I love its implacable calmness, its unwillingness to give its secrets away. It's a puzzle that cannot be solved, isn't supposed to be solved, because it is in the process of grappling with it that we discover the point for ourselves. Every time I have read the novel has been prismatic, opening up reflections on cruelty, on human nature, on capitalism. Reading it is not a passive experience but one that provokes, that exasperates, that moves.

If there is an essential message in a book full of such truth, the following sentence is a good place to take it from: 'I was forced to acknowledge too late, much too late, that I too had loved, that I was capable of suffering, and that I was human after all', our narrator muses at the start of the novel, as her life draws to an end. Then shortly afterwards, 'After all, if I was a human being, my story was as important as that of King Lear, or of Prince Hamlet that William Shakespeare had taken the trouble to relate in detail.' The smallness of one person left alive in the vast and mysterious world is a daunting concept. But doesn't the best science fiction make us think about our world anew, and who we are? If the narrator has lived a life as best as she could—wildly unconventional, but one that has given her joy in many ways—hasn't she triumphed over cruelty after all, over having everything stripped from her, her dignity and essential humanity winning in the end?

Sophie Mackintosh
2019

JACQUELINE HARPMAN was born in Etterbeek, Belgium, in 1929. Her family fled to Casablanca when the Nazis invaded, and only returned home after the war. After studying French literature she started training to be a doctor, but could not complete her training due to contracting tuberculosis. She turned to writing in 1954 and her first work was published in 1958. In 1980 she qualified as a psychoanalyst. Harpman wrote over 15 novels and won numerous literary prizes, including the Prix Médicis for *Orlanda*. *I Who Have Never Known Men* was her first novel to be translated into English, and was originally published with the title *The Mistress of Silence*. Harpman died in 2012.

ROS SCHWARTZ has translated numerous works of fiction and non-fiction from French, including several Georges Simenon titles for Penguin Classics, a new translation of Antoine de Saint-Exupéry's *The Little Prince* and, most recently, Mireille Gansel's *Translation as Transhumance*. The recipient of a number of awards, she was made a Chevalier de l'Ordre des Arts et des Lettres in 2009 and received the Institute of Translation and Interpreting's John Sykes Memorial Prize for Excellence in 2017.

Transit Books is a nonprofit publisher of international and American literature, based in Oakland, California. Founded in 2015, Transit Books is committed to the discovery and promotion of enduring works that carry readers across borders and communities. Visit us online to learn more about our forthcoming titles, events, and opportunities to support our mission.

TRANSITBOOKS.ORG